Glenda
yours truly my

Speak Now Or...
Hold Your Piece

Pleasure.
Live, Love, Laugh

A Novel By
Lonnie B. Spry

Copyright © 2010 Lonnie Spry
All rights reserved

Without limiting the copyright reserved above, no part of this publication may be reproduced, stored in or introduced into a retrieval system, or transmitted, in any form, or by any means (electronic, mechanical, photocopying, recording, or otherwise), without prior written permission of both copyright owner and the above publisher of this book.

PUBLISHER'S NOTE
This is a work of fiction. Names, characters, places, and incidents either are the product of the author's imagination or are used fictitiously, and any resemblance to actual persons, living or dead, events, or locales is entirely coincidental.

ISBN-13: 978-1-4507-3524-7

Editor/Typesetter: Carla M. Dean, U Can Mark My Word
Book Cover: Brian Thompson, B. Design Firm
Photo of Author: Montell Williams, Sharp Image Studios

ACKNOWLEDGEMENTS

First and foremost, I would like to give praise and thanks to my Lord and Savior Jesus Christ, because through him all things are possible.

I would like to acknowledge my wife, Tonya. Thank you for all of your support. To my mother, Dorothy Colbert, thanks for always being there for me. To my daughters, Erin and Michaela, I love you both. I may not be the best father in the world, but I will keep trying.

I would also like to acknowledge my aunt, Joanne Martin (I love you, Auntie), my father Lonnie B. Spry, Sr., Shavon and Orren Mingo, Tyrena Spry, Timothy (Tim Dawg) Spry, Gabrielle "Gabbie" Sherrod. A special thanks to Truman "TJ" Martin, Altovese and TC Warner, Jennifer "Yella Gurl" Martin, James and Traci Warner, Richard "Big Rick" Colbert, Aunt Germaine Hubbard, Dana Hubbard, Harriet Bell, Joseph Bell and T'Wana Warrick-Bell, and Joseph "Jo-Jo" Warrick-Bell.

My main apple scrapples: Geoffrey Adams, Darryl and Tara Jordan, Lorenzo Watson, Sherrell and Tolaundo King, Robert and Lisa Smith, Lori Kearse (We always got Carrabas), Mark and Meryl Irish, Sheila Bunn, Alexis Pate, Tere Meads, Essence Morris, Carl and Angela Cameron, Jocelyn Lawson (Thank you), Naloe Ervin (Thank you), Yonder (You always know which way to guide me in my writing career), and The Sweet Soul Sisters Book Club.

I also want to give a special shout out to my editor, Carla M.

Lonnie Spry

Dean (www.ucanmarkmyword.com), Sylver Logan Sharp (You have to get her album at www.sylverwear.com), Demarco Solar (www.demarcosolar.com), We R One (www.weronegear.com), Gerald Wilson, and Monica Pleasant.

Lastly, for my loved ones who can't be here to help me celebrate this accomplishment, Truman "Pop" Martin (You helped make me the man that I am), Lillie Mae Lawson, Robert Spry, Barbara Jean Nesbitt, Robert Colbert Sr., and Wayne Bagby, I will mourn you until I join you.

To anyone I forgot, charge it to my head and not to my heart. Thank you all for your support.

Speak Now Or...
Hold Your Piece

It Was All a Dream

The stranger walked towards Elbee hard and fast. Elbee knew that murderous look in his eyes because he had seen it many times while growing up in Capitol Heights, Maryland. He didn't know what the stranger's problem was, but if he needed help solving it, Elbee knew he was up to the task. Standing tall, he stared at the stranger as he prepared himself for whatever drama was going to come.

"Main man, you got something that belongs to me."

"Dude, I don't even know who the hell you are," Elbee retorted, while clenching his fists and adjusting his stance.

"What's mine is mine and will always be mine, Slim," the stranger barked, then pulled a nine millimeter handgun from his waist.

"Dawg, I don't even know who you are, and I definitely don't know what it is of yours that I have. Let me know what it is and I might give it back."

"I don't need you to give me anything, punk. I'll take what's mine," the stranger snapped.

"Whatever, dude. You can say what you want, but I still don't know what I got that belongs to you, and with you having that gun in my face, I don't care. So, you do what you gotta do, but I ain't going out like no sucka," Elbee continued through clenched teeth, stepping towards the stranger.

Realizing that Elbee was not going to back down, the stranger began to squeeze the trigger. "You have my…"

Elbee heard a loud bang and jumped up out of a deep sleep. He sat on the bed dripping with sweat and feeling all over his 5'10", 220-pound frame for gunshot wounds. It was all a dream, but it seemed too real. He could even mentally see the man's face.

"What's wrong, baby?" Angel asked, as she watched Elbee rub all over his torso.

Elbee found it hard to believe he was just dreaming. With everything being so real, he wondered if it was more of a vision or premonition than a dream. If it was a vision, who was the guy and what did he have that belonged to him.

"Everything is cool. I just had a bad dream, but I'm aw'ight, though. What are you doing up?"

"Boy, you woke me up, and the word is alright."

"Angel, *boy* is a white racist word, and why you always on a brotha about how he speaks? Am I or am I not on point when I stand in front of those white boys at work?"

"I must admit, you do have those good ole boys eating out of your hand. But, you still should try to speak proper English more often."

"Woman, stop all that fussin'. Oh, my bad, fussing. Now, come on over here so Big Daddy can put you back to sleep."

Angel slid closer to Elbee, and in her sexiest voice whispered, "Do what you do, Big Daddy."

Elbee grabbed Angel and held her in his arms. He was astonished at how soft she always seemed to be. Her smooth, silky skin made loving her and making love to her all the better.

He began kissing Angel on her neck. The moist gentleness of Elbee's lips made her body quiver. Using his tongue to trace the nape of her neck, he caused her body to begin tingling even more. It was as if her clitoris knew she was going to get some special attention because it began throbbing.

Angel had not been with a lot of men sexually, but to her, Elbee was hands down the best. None of the others had been able to make her feel the way he did. She felt that sex with the other guys was a chore, something she had to do to keep the happiness in her relationship. Her girlfriends would always tell her that she was crazy when she would say she didn't enjoy sex. However, that all changed when she met Elbee.

The first time Angel and Elbee were to have sex, she was dreading every moment of it. She knew if she wanted to keep her man happy she had to endure that part of the relationship, but she was still hesitant. What she received that night was more than what she bargained for because she had never experienced the joy, pleasure, or orgasmic feelings she felt with Elbee.

She couldn't understand how being with the men in her other relationships made her tense up, but just the thought of being with Elbee made her moist. Even when he wasn't around, just the thought of sex with Elbee got her panties wet.

Elbee began to lick on Angel's breast. He thought she had some of the most beautiful breasts he had ever seen, and he had seen quite a few. To Elbee, Angel's breasts were perfect. They weren't that big, but, as Elbee's grandfather would always say, 'more than a mouthful was a waste'. They were definitely a mouthful. Just looking at her caramel-colored breasts with milk chocolate nipples excited him and made his mouth water.

Slowly and with extreme precision, Elbee used his tongue to lick Angel from her breasts to her navel, where he circled it slowly and sensuously. Then he licked from her navel to her left inner thigh. After leaving a passion mark on her inner thigh, he licked down her leg until he got to her perfectly manicured toes.

As he licked the bottom of Angel's foot, he could hear her start to moan. Whenever he heard that sound, he knew he was hitting a hot spot and pleasing her. So, he began talking to her.

"Is this what you like, baby?" he asked, while sucking on her toes.

"You know I like that, but I want to feel your dick inside me," she moaned.

Angel would have never talked dirty before she met Elbee. When she would have sex, she would just lay there like Mrs. Celie in the *Color Purple* and let her man do his business. The difference between Elbee and the other guys was that he made love to her mind before he ever touched her body.

Elbee was more concerned about Angel's pleasure than his own. So, when she told him that she had never had an orgasm, he made it his mission to help her achieve that goal. He purchased a Karma Sutra book and volumes 1 and 2 of Yonder's *What I Do Is Taboo* for her to read. Before they had sex, he wanted her to imagine how wonderful it could be. When they did have sex for the first time, Angel knew then that Elbee was the last man she wanted to ever enter her sugar walls.

Elbee had ignored Angel's request for penetration as he started to move up her right leg, licking every inch while simultaneously using his finger to caress the lips of her womanhood. Then, just as she began to feel the volcano inside her start to rumble, he started tongue kissing the center of her passion. He used his tongue to explore her insides and his thick, full lips to rub her clitoris. After about four minutes of intense oral stimulation, Angel exploded with ecstasy.

"Damn, baby, you got a brotha's face lookin' like a glazed donut," Elbee quipped with a snicker.

Through deep breaths and body shivers, she replied, "That's your fault. You know how what you did makes me feel. Now stop playing and finish what you started."

Elbee and Angel made love for a half hour before falling off to sleep. As Elbee dozed off, all he could do was think about the big day he had in front of him and how his life had changed for the better.

Special Lady

"You have a collect call from Rocky Barnes at Central State Prison. Please press five to accept this call," the voice recording said.

Rocky was in prison in Macon, Georgia after being found guilty by a jury of his peers. He was sentenced to twenty-five years in prison for drug trafficking. Since the car he was driving wasn't registered to him, the district attorney had a problem connecting it to him. That was until the worker that Rocky had with him the day he was arrested decided to testify for the prosecution in exchange for a lighter sentence.

"What's up, Rock? How you holding up in there? You ain't drop the soap, did you?" Tony said, laughing.

"Ha-ha, very funny, motherfucka. Is Pop around, ya bastard?"

"Naw, he's gone to speak with your lawyer about trying to get you out."

"What is the lawyer saying?" Rocky queried.

"From what your pops was telling me, there is a good

chance you might be home soon. As for right now, we have a few people that we have to terminate and a few people we have to hire."

Rocky knew exactly what Tony was saying. Rocky's father had to have the worker that testified against Rocky killed and pay off the district attorney. Tony and Rocky knew the phones in the prison were monitored, so they made sure they spoke in code.

"Tony, have the boys been keeping an eye on Angel?"

"Well, let me see. How can I put this? Aaaaah, no. Them dummies lost her."

"What the hell do you mean they lost her? How the fuck do you lose a grown damn person when your only job is to keep tabs on them?"

Tony dropped his head as if Rocky was standing in front of him. "See, what had happened was your father had a problem with the neighbors, so he had me pull everybody off everything else to get that together. By the time we settled with the neighbors and started expanding the land, she had disappeared."

"Damn, Tony, I asked you to do one thing and you blew it!" Rocky yelled.

"Rock, what did you want me to do? Tell your pops that I couldn't send the guys that he pays over to help him because they're watching a girl that he told us to leave alone? Like that was really going to happen."

"Yeah, you right," Rocky chuckled. "Boy, if you had told Pops that you still had people watching over Angel after he said not to, he would've had you put your hand on the piano like old boy in *Harlem Nights*.

They both began to laugh at the thought.

"So no one has seen her, huh?" Rocky asked.

"Nope. I even got people keeping an eye on her folks' crib to see if she shows up. She calls them from time to time, but she uses a calling card when she calls. At least that's what I heard. Rock, what is it with this broad? I mean, she's cute and all that, but damn. Hell, you got a bunch of fine bitches trying to get at you, and you stuck on her."

"It's not about how fine she is. Any man can look at a woman and see quantity, but only a real man knows how to spot a woman of quality, a special lady."

"Nigga, is that some jailhouse philosophy bullshit you spittin'?"

"Naw, fool. Pops taught me that. See what happens when you don't have a man around. Listen to Pops when he talks and you'll learn something."

"I hear what you saying, Rock. So what do you want me to do about Angel?" Tony questioned.

"Reach out to her brother Onesimus. Have him tell you where she is, and if he has a problem with that, kindly remind him of the bill he owes."

"Gotcha, boss. When I find her what should I do?"

"Just have someone watch out for her 'til I get home. I want to make sure she's safe."

"What should I do if she's seeing someone? Should I have a talk with him?"

"No. If she's seeing someone, just get the low down on him and I will handle that when I get home. Aw'ight, dude, I gotta go before I have to knock the CO out. I'll holla."

"Peace out, homie, and keep your head up."

Three P's

The winter air blowing in Elbee's face had him wide awake. He had been finding it harder and harder to get out of bed in the mornings. The dreams he had been having were keeping him up and making him a little more paranoid than he usually was.

Elbee sat in his truck, said a quick prayer, and pulled out of the driveway heading to work. Once he was on the road, he went through the radio stations for something to listen to. He would have normally listened to some Jay-Z, Nas, Scarface, or Kanye West to get him prepared for his daily grind. Today was different, though. For some strange reason, he felt the need to listen to the radio.

He had gone through a couple of stations when he came across the Steve Harvey Morning Show on 96.3 WHUR. He had heard so much about the show that he just tuned in and listened.

Elbee had been a fan of Steve Harvey from the first time

that he saw him on *Def Comedy Jam*. He followed his career from his short-lived sitcom *Me and the Boys* to *The Steve Harvey Show*, and you couldn't tell Elbee that Steve's routine on *The Kings of Comedy Tour* wasn't a classic. Every time he went to church one of the older women would remind Elbee of Sister Odell, and just like Steve's church, his had a building fund but nothing had been changed.

Steve and Nephew Tommy had been through a couple of skits that had Elbee crying from laughter. What happened next gave Elbee something to think about. It was the segment of the show called "Ask Steve". This was when the callers got to ask Steve questions and he would give them his opinion.

The first caller asked Steve why he thought her boyfriend wouldn't marry her even though they had been together for five years and had two children together. Steve responded by telling her that a man will only do what a woman lets him do. He continued by letting her know that as long as he was able to have the milk without buying the cow, he was going to do so.

Elbee was shaking his head in agreement as he drove along the highway thinking how deep the answer was. He remembered his grandmother saying the same thing to him when he was growing up, and he had found it to be so true.

The next caller, who was also female, wanted to know why men cheat even though they claim they love you. Once again, Steve was up to the challenge when confronted with the question. He promptly let the young lady know that just because a man cheats it doesn't mean he doesn't love you. He went on to say that, for men, it was about the physical act and not the emotion when they were cheating. That was why a man could cheat and still say he loved his woman.

When the next caller was queued up, it was also a woman. Elbee started to wonder if any brothers were going to call in. After teasing the young lady about her name, Steve let her ask her question. The young lady, Sequoia, told Steve that she had been with her friend for six months, and now he was telling her that he loved her. She wanted to know how she could be sure.

Steve proceeded to let her know that if a man really loved her that he would display the three P's. Elbee had heard and learned a lot about relationships in his thirty odd years of living, but he hadn't heard about the three P's. So, instead of getting out of his SUV when he pulled into his parking space at Beltek Technologies, he sat listening intently to the knowledge that Steve was about to drop.

Steve informed the young lady that when a man truly loves a woman, he will *profess* his love for her. He will *protect* her, and he will *provide* for her. That statement hit Elbee like a ton of bricks. For the statement to be so simple it was so extremely profound.

After hearing Steve expound on the three P's, it caused Elbee to reflect on his relationship with Angel. He began to ask himself if he had shown her that he would provide for her and protect her while professing his love for her.

At that moment, Elbee knew what he needed to do without question. Without hesitation, he pulled out his cell phone, pressed seven, and listened to the phone ring.

"Good morning. Government Printing Office. Rhonda Barnes speaking."

"Hey, Rhonda, this is Elbee. I need your help with something."

Orientation

Angel sat at her desk slumped over, sleepy and barely able to keep her eyes open. She knew she needed to speak with Elbee concerning his nightmares. Something had to be done immediately, or else he couldn't stay with her on weeknights. Angel was beginning to nod again, when she heard a knock on her office door.

"Good morning, Ms. Terry. The new hires are in the conference room," the intern announced.

"Okay, Tatianna, I will be right out as soon as I get some coffee."

"Is there anything you need me to do?"

"If you could pass out the new hire packets, I would appreciate that. Could you also pass out these technical performance evaluation contracts?"

Angel stood up and stretched. She was not looking forward to overseeing this new hire orientation. *Elbee is supposed to be handling these rednecks from Telecom Technologies*, she thought, but at the last minute, he found out that he had to go to closing on his property.

"What's going on, Angel?" Blak inquired, tapping on her office door.

"Oh hey, Blak. I'm getting ready to do this new hire orientation, for the telecom technicians we brought over in the merger."

"Okay, cool. Hey, I thought Elbee was supposed to be doing that? Where is he today?"

With sarcasm in her voice, she replied, "That Ms. Hawkins called at the last minute and said she scheduled him to go to closing on his property today. So, he rushed right out of here to meet her. Blak, I can't stand that wench."

"Okay, now tell me how you really feel," Blak said, while laughing. "Elbee said she's good at her job. That's why I was planning on using her as my realtor."

"Yeah right, and Carolyn will be looking at you like you missed snack time. Like ole boy on that McDonald's commercial."

They both laughed.

"Now why would you say something like that?"

"Blak, that heifer has been flirting with Elbee through this whole ordeal. Elbee is just so enamored with her work that he can't see it."

"Is she flirting or just being friendly?"

"Friendly, flirting...what's the damn difference? They both start with an 'F'."

"Girl, you're a nut."

There was a knock on the door.

"Ms. Terry, they're ready," the intern reminded her.

"I'll be there in a moment," Angel answered. "Well, Blak, I

gotta go welcome the good ole boy network to the company."

"Aw'ight, you go do that. I'm going to hit Elbee on his cell. Oh and Angel?"

"Yes, Blak."

"You have fun now. Ya hear? Yeee hawww!"

"Bye, boy."

•

Temptation

"Congratulations, Mr. Nessprin. You are now the proud owner of a ten-unit apartment building."

Elbee could not believe his ears when he heard his real estate agent say those words. He had been back and forth for several months trying to get financed so he could purchase the building, but he kept getting denied. Although he had finally made it to the big leagues in corporate America and was making six figures, the bankruptcy he had on his credit report was truly hurting him.

Elbee didn't want to file bankruptcy when he started back to work, but his new financial advisor felt that he should. So, he followed her advice when she said it would be the best way for him to get back on track financially. After being turned down by several mortgage lenders, he wasn't so sure the information he had received was correct. He was so frustrated that he contacted his financial advisor, Karen Early, hoping to obtain some better advice. She in turn directed him to real estate agent

Pamela Hawkins.

Pamela Hawkins was gorgeous. There was no other way to explain it. When Elbee first saw her, he almost broke his neck doing a double take. Pamela was PHAT, pretty hot and tempting. Elbee stood looking at Pamela as he thought, *She is phatter than four horses, three cows, two mules, and a chia-pet.*

The thing about her that really turned Elbee on was the delicate mole slightly to the left of her top lip. He could vividly imagine his tongue rolling over it. He eyed Pamela's shapely legs with the hair on them. Then thought, *DAMN! She is sexy as hell.*

Not only was Pamela easy on the eyes, she was also a beast at what she did. Once she had thoroughly reviewed Elbee's paperwork, credit history, and bank account, she found that he had quickly saved ten thousand dollars when he began working. Impressed, she became determined to help him get his loan. The fact that every time Elbee licked his thick, full lips she became moist added to her determination.

"Mrs. Hawkins, when we first met, you told me that you could work miracles. Well, all I have to say is you did your thing and I thank you for the miracle."

"First of all, Mr. Nessprin, it's *Ms.* Hawkins," she said, emphasizing the Ms., "but it's Pamela if you're nasty."

Elbee smiled so she wouldn't notice that he was blushing. Ms. Hawkins had been so professional throughout the whole process that he wasn't sure if she was flirting or just playing. Therefore, he just ignored the statement.

"Do you have the keys to the building, Ms. Hawkins?"

"Yes, I do, Mr. Nessprin," she replied, teasingly twirling them around her finger. "But I would like to ask you one question before I give them to you."

"Sure, go ahead," he replied, while slipping the keys off of her finger.

"Of all the units I showed you, why did you pick this one? It needs so much work."

"Well, Ms. Hawkins, the building is in the neighborhood that I grew up in, and I have some very fond memories of that neighborhood."

"Like what?" she asked with a look of disgust on her face.

"Well, you may not believe it, but when I was younger, the people in that neighborhood truly believed it took a village to raise a child. The lady up the street, Mrs. Mary, beat me because she heard me cursing and then told my mother who beat me again. The guy down the street, Mr. Wailer, coached football for the Boys and Girls Club. All the boys in the neighborhood who wanted to play football played for that club. He would transport all us back and forth in his van to practice and games whether we played for him or not. So, I want to help rebuild the place that helped me become the man that I am today. With the county wanting all of these old buildings fixed up, it will be easy to get permits for the renovations I have planned."

"The permits thing sounds good. Now back to the memories. Are those the only ones you have?"

"Nope, I had my first sexual encounter in that neighborhood," Elbee responded with a silly grin.

"Now I would love to hear about that," Ms. Hawkins said as she moved closer to Elbee and seductively removed the keys from his grip.

The scented oil Pamela Hawkins was wearing was so

enticing that Elbee could barely think straight. In his mind, he could see himself closing the door to the conference room and ravaging her right there on the conference table.

"There ain't much to tell. It only lasted about thirty seconds," Elbee replied.

"How long can you go now?" Pamela blurted with a devilish grin, placing the keys on the conference table.

Pamela could see Elbees's mind at work. She could tell he was contemplating giving her everything that she had wanted since the first day she laid eyes on him. The first time Pamela met Elbee, he was coming from the gym. She had called to remind him of their meeting, and he didn't have a chance to go home and change. He was wearing a Kevin Durrant jersey and some mesh basketball shorts. It was at that point she wanted to be in his muscular arms, and it was also when she realized the scented oil she liked to wear, Pussy, had a big effect on Elbee.

The minute Elbee got a whiff of the oil, Elbee Jr. stood at attention, and no matter how much he tried to hide it, he couldn't. From that moment on, Pamela wanted to dance with his one-eyed monster. She felt that Angel attending the rest of their meetings ruined her chances, though. Knowing Angel wouldn't be at the closing, Pamela wore her fragrance, hoping to be able to seduce Elbee into one night of infidelity.

Pamela leaned in closer to Elbee to make sure he could smell her Pussy, and when she did, she could see his nature rise. The heat from her breath caused Elbee's manhood to pulsate even more. It felt as if all the blood was leaving the rest of his body and running to his penis.

Elbee's mind had gone blank. The only thing he could think of was bending Pamela over the conference room table. As much as he tried to fight the feeling, the temptation was just too strong. While Elbee began to reach for Pamela, his cell phone rang, saving him from himself.

"Hello!"

The Rock

Rocky walked back to his cell on an emotional high. He knew when his father wanted things done, they got done. So, he knew it was just a matter of time before he was back on the streets.

Rocky Espananza was born Rocky Barnes. His father named him Rocky because of his love for Sylvester Stallone. Rocky was the epitome of tall, dark, and handsome. He was so dark that the only difference between him and midnight was about thirty seconds. He would have been just another dark-skinned brother if it wasn't for the fact that he had gray eyes. Women loved him for his eyes, but men saw him as cold, dangerous, and extremely deadly.

After his biological father stabbed his mother to death and beat him within an inch of his life when he was twelve years old, he was placed in foster care. Even as an adult, he still had some of the physical scars from the beating, although his most damaging scars were emotional.

It wasn't alcohol or drugs that caused Rocky's father to be

abusive. Jealousy was the reason his father flew into terrible fits of rage. Rocky's mother quit her job hoping the beatings would stop. Family and friends tried desperately to get her to leave, but she always rebuffed them while reciting the words "Til Death Do Us Part" from her marriage vow.

When Rocky was fifteen, he became tired of the mental and physical abuse from his foster parents, so he ran away. That's when he started working for Ricardo Espananza, the biggest drug dealer in New York. Needing money for food and shelter, he became a low-level runner for Ricardo.

One day while in the corner store, Rocky overheard a rival dealer concocting a plan to kill Ricardo. Rocky knew this information would help him move up in Ricardo's organization. So, he did everything he could to find out how the plan was supposed to work without being detected.

Once Rocky knew the plan, he made a beeline straight to Ricardo's headquarters to lay out the plan he had overheard. Ricardo listened to Rocky lay out the scheme that was made to take his life, and then he thanked Rocky.

Things happened just the way Rocky had laid it out but with a different ending. When the shooting stopped, instead of Ricardo being killed, he was the one left standing. Not only did he take out the rival dealer, he also gained control of his territory.

Wanting to show his appreciation, Ricardo reached into his pocket and handed Rocky a thousand dollars.

Handing Ricardo back the money, Rocky told him, "Thank you for the money, Ricardo, but I did what I did because we're a family."

Realizing Rocky wanted and needed more than money,

Ricardo looked at the young man that wanted his acceptance and called him son.

Ricardo then looked at his lieutenants and proclaimed, "From this day forth, Rocky will no longer be a runner but my son. Rocky Barnes is no more. Today, Rocky Espananza a.k.a. the Rock is born."

Ricardo looked at Rocky, "When I eat, you eat. Where I lay my head, you will lay your head."

Now the last thing Ricardo had to do was take care of his traitorous wife.

Ricardo looked at Rocky, "Okay, Rock, to make your adoption complete there is something you must do."

"Anything, Ricardo."

Ricardo looked at his wife and handed Rocky his gun.

"Kill this BITCH!"

Rocky took the gun, closed his eyes, and without hesitation, he pulled the trigger.

"Espananza, you got a visitor," the guard yelled, bringing Rocky back to reality.

Rocky smiled brightly as he got to the visitor center and saw Deshawn, Angel's best friend. She would know how to find Angel.

No Drama

"Hello, Mr. Brown. How may I help you, sir?" Elbee stammered, while looking at Pamela.

Pamela began undoing her blouse, while Elbee looked on trying not to succumb to his desires.

"So you need me to come into the office? Okay, sir, I will be there in twenty minutes."

Elbee closed his cell phone, told Pamela he had to go, grabbed the keys for his building, and practically ran out of the door. He was totally confused. On the one hand, Pamela Hawkins was the type of woman that most men would want to sleep with and she was literally throwing the coochie at him. On the other hand, Angel was just as beautiful and he loved her. The thought of hurting Angel was enough to make Elbee get into his SUV and speed off.

Elbee had just pulled out of the parking lot, when his cell phone rang again.

"Holla at ya boy."

"What the hell is this *Mr. Brown* shit?" Blak asked.

Kim Brown a.k.a. Blak had been Elbee's boy since they were in the seventh grade. He was also the reason that Elbee was the Director of Telephony for Beltek Technologies, making Blak his boss, which is why the staff meetings were always off the hook.

"Man, you would not believe what the hell just happened to me, fool."

"What happened?" Blak shot back.

"You remember my real estate agent, Pamela Hawkins?"

"You mean that fine one?"

"Yeah, man."

"Okay, what about her?"

"Dawg, she just tried to fuck me on her conference room table."

"Stop playin'. She's going like that?"

"If you had called about two minutes later, I would have been beating them guts up."

"Oh, my bad, dude."

"Naw, man, I owe you one. I don't need to be getting caught up in no bullshit. I love my baby, and like Mary J Bilge, I don't want any drama in my life."

"So do you own the building now or what, fool?"

"And you know this, mannn," Elbee responded, trying to sound like Chris Tucker.

"That means you'll be moving outta my house soon so I can run around the house butterball-butt-ass-naked," Blak replied, laughing.

"That's just T.M.I., dawg. But, yeah, I'll be moving as soon as possible."

"Brotha, you know you're welcome as long as you need a place to stay. Hey, what's that I hear you pumping?"

"I picked up this CD called *Place to Begin* by a local artist named Sylver Logan Sharp. Man, this thang is bangin'."

"That joint hot like that? I might have to borrow that thang."

"Where are you on your way to now?"

"I'm on my way to meet Benny to give him the keys to the building so him and his boys can start renovating my spot. Then, I'm going to hook up with Rhonda so she can help me with a mission."

"Well, tell that nigga Benny I said what's up."

"Aw'ight then, fool."

"I'll get up. Peace."

Signed, Sealed, and Delivered

Angel sat at her desk feeling mentally drained. She couldn't understand how some people could be such assholes. *That's okay,* she thought. *They may have gotten me today, but I'll get them in the long run.*

The telephone ringing brought her back to the tasks at hand.

"Beltek Technologies, this is Angel."

"Hello, Angel. How are you today?"

"I am fine. How may I help you?"

"I was wondering if you could tell me what color panties you're wearing."

"Who is this?"

"I'm asking the questions, and I want to know what color panties you're wearing?"

"Who is this?"

"Now is this any way to treat an old friend?"

Angel's heart began beating fast. This couldn't be who she thought it was. *How did he find me?* she thought. *How did he get my number?*

"Why so quiet? Don't you know what color panties you're wearing? If that's too hard of a question, then how about letting me suck on your nipples? Why don't I just come on over and get a taste of those chocolate-covered nipples."

"You better stay away from me. If my boyfriend finds out who you are, he's going to be all over you."

"Fuck that red nigga! I'll beat his ass!" the caller exclaimed, and then started to snicker.

"Boy, you play too much, and I know that *boy* is a white racist word."

"You catch on pretty quick," Elbee said through his laughter. "How's your day going, sweetie?"

"Besides the fact that my wonderful, truly childish boyfriend left me alone all day with some cranky, old white guys, then called and scared me into thinking I had a crazy stalker, I am okay."

"Did those old, cranky white guys sign the performance agreements?"

"Most of them did. Some of them complained and said they weren't going to sign them. However, once they found out their jobs were contingent on them signing on the dotted line, they did it."

When Elbee came up with the idea to keep everyone on at the same rate of pay and then terminate them later, he had to make sure he had all of his ducks in a row. So, he put together a set of performance parameters that they all needed to meet and verified everything through the legal department. He knew the people that he wanted to get rid of would be working so hard to make him look bad that they would forget about meeting their performance objectives.

"Good, good, good. Now that the papers are signed, sealed, and delivered, let the games begin."

"Elbee, this is not a game. What if these guys do what they are supposed to do? You could lose your job."

"Angel, honey, there are two things that I know in this world. They are my job and people. So, just trust me. Those fools hate me so bad that they are going to dig their own hole, and when they do, I'll be there to push their asses in."

"Okay, trust me. Well, I have to go. Carolyn just walked into my office."

"Aw'ight, applehead. I'm going to meet Benny at my new home."

"Your mother is an applehead. Bye."

Today Was a Good Day

Elbee pulled up in front of the property that he had just purchased. As he looked at the building he was going to renovate and turn into some nice apartments that would be a good investment, he knew he had to thank God for his favor. If he didn't already believe that all things were possible through God, he sure would believe it now.

A car pulled into the parking spot next to Elbee. He didn't have a clue as to who was driving the S500 Mercedes Benz with tinted windows and sitting on 22-inch chrome rims. The one thing he did know was that the car was off the hook.

Elbee sat in his truck waiting to see who was going to get out of the Benz, but nothing happened. After the dreams Elbee had been having, he began to get a little nervous. So, he slowly reached for his gun. Elbee had made it up in his mind if he had to go, he was going to go fighting. Just as he grabbed the nickel-plated glock nine millimeter handgun that was lodged under his seat, the window of the Benz rolled down.

"Get your hand off that gun, fool. I don't know why you got

it because you ain't gonna shoot nobody," Elbee's cousin Benny said, laughing.

Benny, born Benjamin Franklin Nessprin, was Elbee's first, older, and favorite cousin. He was tall with a cocoa complexion, hazel eyes, and a muscular physique he had obtained while incarcerated.

Benny's senior year in high school started out with him being the number two rated basketball player in the country. In the neighborhood, he was a basketball icon. He was being courted by schools like Temple University, University of Michigan, USC, and some others, but Benny said he could only play for a hometown team. So, he signed a letter of intent to play for the Georgetown Hoyas. A few days after Benny signed his letter of intent, he was at the bus stop waiting for the bus, when his best friend pulled up in a nice Nissan 300Z and told him to hop in. Before Benny knew what was going on, the police were chasing them, and during the chase, a sixteen-year-old girl was hit and killed. Although Benny's friend took all of the blame for the car and accident, the state's attorney wanted to send a message to teenagers stealing cars and prosecuted Benny, also. Benny served three years in prison, losing his scholarship and any chance to play professional basketball. He was never the same after losing what meant the world to him, which was his chance to play basketball for the world to see. It didn't help any that Elbee quit playing basketball after Benny got incarcerated, giving up any chances for him to go to college, too.

Elbee stuck his gun back under the seat. "Man, you play too damn much. I was sho'nuff ready to put a hot one in yo' ass."

"Nigga, please, you wasn't gonna do shit with yo' punk

ass," Benny joked, as he stepped out of the car wearing a blue and gray DeMarco Solar sweat suit.

"Damn, you ballin', huh? That sweat suit is hot. I see you been over there talking to Big D. I need to go holla at him myself and pick me up a couple shirts and thangs."

"Well, you know I gotta be top flight. The people know me in these here parts."

"Yeah yeah yeah. Whatever, nigga. So the gear is yours, but who car you done stole?"

"Well, if you must know, I got a little cousin who helped me get a small business loan. He also gave me my first home improvement project, so I leased me a car. Hell, the boss can't be riding the bus."

Elbee got out of his truck, walked over to his cousin, and gave him some dap. "Boy, you is off the hook. The car is cool as long as my spot is finished in six months like you promised in our contract."

"If it's not, what you gonna do, whip my ass?" Benny asked, laughing.

Benny was two years older than Elbee, but when Elbee moved to Capitol Heights from Georgia, he took Elbee under his wing. Benny taught Elbee how to dress, how to fight, and how to meet girls. Benny taught Elbee everything he learned from his father and their uncles.

"No, I'm not going to whip your ass. What I am going to do is call your mother," Elbee asserted as they both laughed.

"So the spot is all yours now, huh, lil' cuz?"

"Yeah, Benny, this is my new home," Elbee answered with happiness in his voice.

"Well, I must say I'm proud of you, fool. You just don't

know how bad it hurt me when I found out you had stopped playing basketball after I got locked up. I have been through things that I never want you to go through, and no matter what it takes, I will not let you go through it," Benny vowed, looking at his little cousin with adoration in his eyes. "The fellas and I will start on the work tomorrow. I got the plans from Ramon earlier today. I sat talking to that boy for a minute, and he's a fool."

"Well, that's Mon for you. You know all of them still see you as The Man."

"Baby boy, I'm just glad none of y'all followed in my footsteps."

"While I got you here, help me put this sign up in the front. I need to let people know that the building is being renovated and who to contact for rental applications," Elbee told Benny.

"Just 'cause you writing the check doesn't mean you can tell me what to do. I am still the oldest and will knock you out. Remember that."

"You just remember if you touch me, I'm telling your mother," Elbee responded as they began to laugh. Elbee looked down at his watch. "Hey, Benny, I have a few more runs to make, so I'm going to get out of here. Here are the keys so you and your team can get to work."

"Okay, we might start tomorrow, but give me a call later."

Elbee jumped into his car and pulled out of the parking lot feeling good. Not only did he own the building, but he was able to do what Shanté did for him. He was able to give his cousin some work.

He rode down the street feeling like Ice Cube, thinking today was a good day.

Have You Seen Her

Deshawn began to get nervous as she sat waiting to see Rocky. She was hoping she didn't see anyone else she knew. Everyone knew she and Angel were best friends. They also knew Angel was Rocky's wife.

Deshawn couldn't believe she was getting involved with Rocky. Angel had always been there for her when she needed someone, and she had been more of a family to Deshawn than her actual family. Deshawn had been so drawn to the power that Rocky possessed that she slept with him the first night they met.

Initially, Deshawn felt bad about sleeping with Rocky after all of the things that she and Angel had been through together. After Rocky started telling her that he and Angel barely had sex, Deshawn began to rationalize what she was doing. Angel not being at Rocky's trial just solidified how Deshawn felt, especially since she was there everyday. She even cried when Rocky was convicted and sentenced. She also made it her business to visit him every week.

"What's up, sexy? It's good to see you."

Deshawn looked into Rocky's shimmering gray eyes and felt butterflies in her stomach. At that moment, she knew exactly what Michael Jackson was singing about. She had often wondered why she still felt so nervous around Rocky after all the times they had made love, but his pearly white smile always made her feel at ease.

"Hi, Rocky. How are you?" she asked, then noticed the bruise on his face. "What happened to your face? Did the guards do that? None of these guys are trying to rape you, are they?" Deshawn questioned with concern.

"Girl, you watch too much TV," Rocky told her through a hearty laugh. "That stuff doesn't really happen for real. Not to me anyway. Plus, everyone knows who my father is, so they don't fuck wit' me. Now where's my hug at?"

When Deshawn gave Rocky a hug, it felt like she was melting in his arms. Rocky didn't smell like the Prada cologne that he wore before he was incarcerated, but she still always liked to smell him. She promised herself this would be the visit that she told him how she felt. Her friendship with Angel was already damaged, so why not totally destroy her marriage and get the man that she wanted?

"Boo, did you get that package from Tony?"

"Yeah."

"Okay, let me get that up off you."

"But the guard is right there. Won't we get in trouble?"

"It's cool. He works for me."

Rocky signaled for the guard to come over. When he got close, Rocky gave him the brown package.

"Go through the normal distribution, except for those Arian bastards. They still owe me money, and they bruised my face and got my baby all worried."

"Cool, Rock. I'll take care of it," the guard replied and walked away.

Rocky stood looking at Deshawn, trying to figure out how he was going to get her to tell him where Angel was. He was sure Deshawn knew where Angel was, but even if she didn't, he was sure she could find her. However, he couldn't come right out and ask her. Although he thought Deshawn was a gold digging slut, he knew she wasn't a dummy. She definitely wasn't going to be played willingly.

Rocky held Deshawn tightly in his arms. She was a beautiful woman, and if he hadn't met Angel first, she might have had a chance. When Rocky felt Deshawn's body go slightly limp, he knew he had her right where he wanted her.

"I've missed holding you like this, kissing your lips, and laying next to you at night," Rocky told her seductively.

"I missed those things, too. I want you home. Rocky, I...I...I love you."

Rocky kissed Deshawn gently on the lips. "I know, boo. I do, too."

Deshawn was in heaven. She finally had someone that she could call her own. She didn't care what Angel or anyone else thought. She would be there until the end for her man. She was going to be the true definition of a ride-or-die chick. Lil' Kim wouldn't have anything on her.

"Rock, I can't wait until you get out of here. I know it's going to be a long twenty-five years, but I will be with you every step of the way."

"That's good, because you're not going to have to wait that long. My pops is working on some things as we speak. So, if everything goes according to plan, I will be out of here in a few months. I'm going to need you to do me a favor before I get out, though."

"Sure, anything."

"I need you to get in touch with Angel and find out where she is. I asked Tony to go see her and he said she moved."

"Why do you need to know where that bitch is?" Deshawn quipped with an attitude. "I thought we were going to be together."

Rocky snatched Deshawn by the arm. "Don't question me. Just do what I say," he snapped.

Deshawn looked at Rocky with fear in her eyes, and he let her arm go.

In a soft, calm voice, Rocky consoled, "Baby, think about it. As long as I'm still tied to Angel, we can't officially be together. That's unless you want me back up in here."

Excitement came over Deshawn. "Ooh Rocky, you really want to be with me?"

"Yeah, I want to be with you, boo. You have been through all of this with me, so why not?"

Deshawn smiled at the thought of being Mrs. Rocky Espanaza. She had often thought about what it would be like to be the wife of such a powerful man. She promised herself that the problems that existed between Rocky and Angel would not come up if Rocky and she were together.

Rocky could see the gleam in Deshawn's eyes. He knew he had her with the promise of marriage. Now, Deshawn would do whatever it would take to find Angel.

"Espananza, time's up!" the guard yelled.

Deshawn kissed Rocky and was off to complete her

mission. If she didn't do anything else, she was going to get in touch with her best friend.

Respeck

Elbee was finding it hard to sleep as he lay in the bed next to Angel. He kept thinking about how he almost slept with Pamela Hawkins, and the excitement from having his own apartment building was overwhelming to him. Since he couldn't sleep, he decided go downstairs and watch TV. As usual, there was nothing on. So, he decided to watch the *Go-Go Live @ the Capital Centre* DVD that he had.

Elbee was seriously reminiscing as he watched DC Scorpio dance back and forth across the stage in his Madness gear while singing "You're a Hustler". He remembered Blak, DB, Ramon and himself partying and having a good time. By the time Chuck Brown hit the stage to do his thing, Elbee had fallen off to sleep.

Elbee was awakened by a cold piece of steel being pressed against his temple. Immediately, he knew it was a gun. His first thought went to Angel.

"Angel!" Elbee yelled.

"Awwww, aren't you such a gentleman? You have a gun

Speak Now Or...Hold Your Piece

pointed at your dome and all you can think about is Angel. Well trust me when I tell you this, there ain't a damn thing you can do to help her. Muthafucka, you got problems of your own. Now get your punk ass up," the stranger snarled.

Elbee rose up off of the couch slowly, trying not to make the stranger antsy. His mind was going a mile a minute. *Who is this dude and what does he want? More importantly, where's Angel?*

The thought of something happening to Angel made Elbee sick. He became nauseated and his knees buckled, but he quickly regained his composure. Elbee knew if he was going to make it out of this situation alive, he couldn't show any sign of weakness. In his mind, he started recalling some of his military training.

The stranger looked in Elbee's eyes to see if there was any fear swirling around in them. "Look at you. You're a scared little bitch."

"I tell you what. Put the gun down and let's see who the bitch is," Elbee shot back, becoming angry. "Where's my girl at, nigga?"

"Who? That slut Angel? Don't worry about her. I'm going to take care of all her needs. Hell, you need to be more concerned about what I'm going to do with your punk ass."

Elbee bit his lip and became calm. "If you hurt my baby, I swear on everything I love that I'm going to kill you, and I'm going to kill you slow."

The stranger started to laugh, but Elbee's calmness unnerved him. So, he smacked Elbee across the face with the barrel of the gun. As Elbee fell to one knee, he could feel the blood gushing into his mouth.

"Nigga, this ain't no movie!" the stranger yelled. "Do you think I'm going to let your bitch ass live? Hell no! What I am going to do, though, is let your ass suffer so that even in your afterlife you will understand to never disrespect me again. So, just know that before you take your last breath you will RESPECK me."

The stranger smacked Elbee with the gun again. The pain he felt was excruciating, but through all of that he couldn't believe he was getting his ass beat by someone who should have been hooked on phonics. He tried to formulate a plan, but the more he tried, the more his head hurt…and the more he couldn't believe the idiot pronounced the word respect with a 'K'.

Elbee lifted himself back up to one knee. He knew if he had any chance of making a move, he had to be in a position to make a quick move. Elbee decided if he could get the stranger talking, then he could distract him just enough to make a move.

Elbee spit the blood out of his mouth. "Dude, you have my attention. Now tell me how I disrespected you."

"You have something that belongs to me and I want it back," the stranger growled as he turned his head.

"Dawg, just let me know what it is that I have of yours and you can have it back. It's not that serious."

"Punk, you can't give me a damn thing!" the stranger stated loudly. "Nigga, I take what I want!"

"My bad, my bad. Calm down and let me know what it is that I have."

Elbee had the stranger talking, which was working into his plan. When he noticed the stranger close his eyes in anticipation of answering the question, Elbee jumped at him.

"You have…"

The stranger opened his eyes in time to see Elbee lunging towards him. At that moment, there was a loud blast and a scream.

Elbee jumped up. It was a dream. He sat on the couch sweating profusely. The dream had terrified him, so he did the only thing he knew to do. He got down on his knees and began to pray.

Happy Hour

"Let a brotha get five shots of Patron," Blak told the bartender.

The bartender walked away for a moment, then came back and poured the five shots.

"That'll be fifty dollars!" the bartender yelled over the music.

Blak gave the young, baby-faced bartender seventy dollars and replied, "Look out for a brotha. I'll be back."

The bartender looked at the twenty-dollar tip he had just received, and with a smile, he said, "No doubt. I got you."

"My man," Blak shot back.

Blak walked over to the table where Ramon, DB, Elbee, and Barron sat laughing, joking, and waiting for their drinks. They had made it their mission to hang out at least once a month, and this was their Friday.

"Tonight, we toast to the fact that come Wednesday of next week I will be getting rid of the good ole boy network and bringing in my boys, giving them promotions with a bump in salary," Elbee boasted.

"I'll drink to that," Blak said. "The way you gave them fools everything they needed to succeed, and still, they found a way to get fired. Elbee, you're one smart mutha."

"Shut yo mouth!" they all said in unison.

"Well, as I heard a man once say, they put themselves in the air. I'm just kicking away the chair," Elbee stated.

The guys sat at the table drinking and eating Buffalo wings until Elbee looked up and saw Blak's old girlfriend walk into the bar.

"Blak, your stalker just walked in the place," Elbee uttered, trying to hold in his laughter.

Everyone turned to see Shawna standing at the entrance looking as good as a steak sandwich to a starving Ethiopian. The deep brown velour Baby Phat sweat suit she was wearing made her chocolate skin glow more than it already did. Shawna looked at Blak, turned her nose up, and kept walking with the guy that she was with.

Barron looked at Blak. "What was that all about?"

"Man, that broad is two sandwiches short of a picnic basket," Blak told him.

"Why you say that, Blak?" Elbee asked, now laughing.

"Aww man, Elbee is laughing. So, there must be a story," DB interjected.

"Hold up. Let me get some more drinks, because if Blak is shaking his head, this is going to be a good one," Ramon joked.

Ramon returned to the table with drinks, sat down, and prepared himself to hear a good story.

"Okay, this is what happened," Blak began. "I know y'all remember when I first started working for the cable company right after college."

All of the guys except for Barron shook their heads yes in acknowledgement.

"Barron, we don't know where the hell you were then, but that's when I met Shawna. Everything was going good. She was nice, caring, understanding, loved football and the Redskins; and to top it all off, she had the bomb wet wet. I was in heaven. That is until I started working a lot of hours with the instant install program the company had going on. That's when I realized Big Daddy was just a little too much for her."

"Fool, we asked you for fact, not fiction," Elbee interrupted, laughing again.

"Fuck you. As I was saying, she was falling in love with a nigga and started tripping out. The final straw was when I was sleep one evening after getting off of work early and felt someone staring at me. I woke up to find that crazy broad looking at me through my bedroom window."

"That doesn't sound that crazy," Barron stated.

"Dawg, that fool was living on the second floor. She was on a ladder. Where the hell did she get a ladder from?" DB elaborated as he laughed hysterically.

The guys were laughing uncontrollably. Being able to laugh at each other's expense somehow strengthened their friendship and the bond they shared.

"What about Elbee's girl?" Blak interjected.

"Who are you talking 'bout?" Elbee asked.

"Ms. Kayla."

"What about Kayla?" Elbee responded.

"Now how you gonna ask what about her. You know what about her, and if you don't, let me refresh your memory. Elbee was kicking it with this chick named Kayla, but they had been beefing all day. Now, of course, we all know how petty Elbee can be, and I knew some drama was going to pop off at the cabaret he was giving that night. So we're at the cabaret having a good damn time, and Kayla showed up at the party expecting to get in for free as usual. Elbee had told his little cousin not to let her in unless she paid for a ticket. So, she was really hot now. Of course, Elbee was walking through the party being Elbee, and the next thing I know Kayla was in the spot drunk and hollering loud as hell, 'Blak, Blak, why your boy trying to fuck my friends?'"

Everyone was laughing and drinking while enjoying the stories being told. Ramon was laughing so hard that he was crying.

"Ramon, you laughing too damn hard for a bama that got me arrested by his ex-girlfriend," Elbee chimed.

"Oh, I got to hear this one," stated Blak.

Elbee sat up in his seat. "Man, this fool was dating this chick named...aahh! I can't think of that crazy heifer's name right now."

"Who you talking 'bout, Trina?" Ramon blurted out.

"Yeah, that's the crazy lady's name. I never did anything to this broad. It was always Ramon's dumb ass."

Blak started to laugh because he could see that Elbee was getting a little frustrated. "So what happened?"

"Okay, I come in from Germany for Christmas, and I wanted to surprise Mom Dukes. So, I call Ramon and ask if he would pick me up from the airport. Blak, you weren't home from school and DB was getting ready for the Orange Bowl. So, of course, since we're boys he said yeah.

"When he picked me up from the airport, he was in this banging Mercedes-Benz E-class. I'm thinking this nigga done came up. As soon as we get in the car, his pager starts going off like crazy. You know how Mon is; he was being all nonchalant, talking about he had to pick somebody up. We get to the police station and ole girl comes out mad as hell, fussing and asking why he was late. Of course, he tells her that he had to pick me up from the airport because I didn't have a ride."

"Well, was I lying? You didn't have a ride, did you?"

DB shook his head. "Ramon, you stupid."

"That's not the bad part. What was bad was she didn't get mad at no-speak-a-no-English ass. She got mad at me."

Twisting his moustache like JJ from *Good Times*, Ramon quipped, "You know, what can I say."

"But why did she lock you up?" Barron inquired.

"I'm getting to that. Now, after the first incident, crazy didn't like me at all, but hey, it's whatever. So that following Friday, I was out with this girl named Sharon and her friend Rhonda. Don't get me wrong. Sharon was nice, but Rhonda was a MONSTER. When I saw her, I realized I was with the wrong one, but it was too late then. Once again, Blak, you were still in Georgia; DB, you already had a Rhonda, but it just so happened that Ramon paged me. Since we were by his house, I decided to just swing by. Why did I do that? Ramon saw Rhonda and forgot all about Hinckley Jr.

"Rhonda and Mon hit it off. So, after getting something to eat and a few drinks, we headed back to Rhonda's house, but on the way there, the daughter of Sam started blowing up Ramon's pager. Now remember, at the time we don't have cell phones. So, I asked that fool what he wanted to do, and of course, he wanted to roll with me.

"When we got to the house, this idiot called Trina and told her that he was with me and I wasn't trying to drop him off."

Laughing, Barron said, "That's why she hemmed you up?"

"Dawg, it gets worse. Trina started asking him where he was so she could come pick him up, and the boy hung up the phone. Then he told her later that I was drunk and cut the phone cord."

"No, he didn't!" DB blurted out.

"Ramon, that was dirty." Barron snickered. "But that still doesn't explain how you got arrested, Elbee."

"Well, right after that, ole girl gave Ramon an ultimatum. Either he stopped hanging with me or they were through. You know what the answer to that was. Then, about two weeks later, she saw me and pulled me over. I wasn't worried until I found out that my cousin had the tags from his BMW on his damn Celica, and off to the big house I went."

Everyone was laughing when the bartender came over to the table with another round of drinks and informed the guys it was last call. They all finished their drinks and decided to go see Rare Essence, the wickedest band alive, at the Classics Nightclub.

Church

The praise team was singing "Because of Who You Are" when Elbee walked through the doors of The Greater New Jerusalem Spirit of Faith Cornerstone Assembly Ebenezer First Missionary Baptist Church of God in Christ of Forestville, Maryland.

Once again, Angel had made him late for church. After being in the military, Elbee had one pet peeve, and it was being late. He especially hated being late for church. He believed that he worshipped an on-time God. So, when it was time to worship Him, Elbee felt he needed to be on time.

When the praise team finished singing, one of the associate ministers stepped up to the podium.

"Let me hear the church say praise the Lord."

The members began clapping and saying praise the Lord.

"Now somebody shout hallelujah," the minister continued.

The minister then proceeded to read a scripture. After he finished, he did something different. Instead of calling on a deacon to pray, he called on Elbee to say a prayer.

Speak Now Or...Hold Your Piece

Elbee was thrown by the request, but he proceeded to the front of the church so he could pray. He stood in front of the congregation and bowed his head.

Let us pray
Lord, I thank you for waking me up today
Which is why I am taking this time to pray
I thank you, Lord, for giving me my health
To me, that's more important than wealth
I know lately I haven't been living right
Yet you still watch over me at night
I've blamed you when times were hard and things went wrong
But I know you used those times to make me strong
When I was afraid and wanted to cry
I felt your embrace as you wiped the tears from my eye
When I was depressed and filled with stress
You sent me an angel to let me see that I was truly blessed
When I ask you about the loved ones that I miss
You told me they were in Heaven having a cookout and playing Bid Whist
I thank you, Lord, for what you have given me
And for watching over my friends and family
Lord, I give you all glory and honor right now as I stand
Because for my life I know you have a plan
I ask for all of my blessings in Jesus' name as I pray
Now I'll say Amen and begin another day
Amen

Elbee completed his prayer and returned to his seat as the service continued on. The offering was lifted, alter call was completed, and it was time for the sermon. As the pastor prepared to preach his message, the choir sang "No Greater Love."

The Reverend Doctor Leon Lonnie Love was the pastor. At first glance, you could tell he was a ladies' man before he became a pastor. Pastor Love was the epitome of a pretty boy, from his curly hair to his hazel brown eyes and his caramel-colored skin tone. He wasn't that tall, but he was handsome and full of charisma.

"Good morning, church," the pastor started. "God is good all the time, and all the time God is good. Church, if you would turn your Bibles with me to Joel the second chapter, we will begin reading at the twenty-eighth verse."

The pastor paused for a second while he waited for the congregation to locate the scripture. As he looked out into the audience, he could see the parishioners looking for the chapter and helping their neighbors find the place in The Good Book.

"Joel is the chapter between Hosea and Amos in the Old Testament for those of you who only read the Bible on Sunday and *Jet Magazine* the rest of the week," the pastor said with a smile, while receiving laughter from the church.

When Pastor Love felt that enough people were with him, he began reading verses twenty-eight through twenty-nine. Then Pastor Love closed his Bible and said, "The word of God for the people of God."

The scripture caught Elbee's attention. The dreams he had been having were starting to trouble him. Maybe something in the sermon would give him some clarity or answers.

"The topic of my sermon today is *Man's Nightmare is God's Dream.*"

A rise of amen's and hallelujahs came from the congregation. Elbee sat asking God to reveal the meaning of the dreams to him.

"Webster defines a dream as a series of thoughts, images, or emotions occurring during sleep, although some of us see dreams as more than that. Some of y'all will have a dream, and instead of asking God for wisdom to understand the dream, we go get Madam Zorra's dream book. Then you head out to the liquor store and play whatever number Madam Zorra says it means."

The pastor threw his handkerchief in the air. "Amen lights!"

Elbee sat motionless as he listened to the minister speak. Hoping to get an understanding of the nightmares he was having, he wondered what God was trying to say to him.

"Church, your dreams are not meant for you to use to get your numbers for the lottery. Madam Zorra can't tell you what a dream means either. It amazes me how my Christian brothers and sisters won't pay their tithes like the Bible says, but will listen to a dream book about what numbers to play for the lottery."

The clapping and amen's could be heard throughout the sanctuary. The congregation wanted Reverend Love to know that he was on point.

"Some time, people, God is using our dreams to get through to us. This ain't *The Color Purple,* but God is trying to tell you something, saints."

The church erupted in praise, amen's, and applause. Reverend Love continued his sermon to the cheers of the members, as Elbee sat still wondering what God was trying to tell him.

Help Mate

Angel sat at her desk going over the numbers for all of the supervisors that Elbee was planning to terminate. She was still amazed at how right he was. She just knew Elbee was going to end up losing his job behind those rednecks, but he proved to be truly smarter than the average bear. The same people that were being given a hard time by their supervisors were the same ones Elbee realized he could count on.

Elbee wanted things to go the way he had planned so bad that he would go out to inspect the technician's work, as well as talk with the customers to see if the technician was being treated fairly. Those that weren't being treated fairly were happy to call Elbee when they needed a supervisor in the field. When Elbee received a call, he would go out to that job site no matter what time it was and wait to see how long it took the supervisor to respond. Elbee had so much paperwork on the ones he wanted to let go it was pathetic.

Speak Now Or...Hold Your Piece

During the whole probationary period, Elbee kept telling Angel that he gave people the rope and they put themselves in the air; he just kicked away the chair. All of the good technicians realized if you did what you were supposed to do, Elbee was your friend, but if you didn't, there were going to be consequences and repercussions.

Angel was so deep in thought that the knock on her door startled her. When she looked up, she saw Carolyn standing in the doorway.

"Carolyn, you scared the mess out of me!" Angel quipped.

"What's going on with you? I haven't seen you all day, and on top of that, you're extremely jumpy."

"Girl, I'm going over these reports for Elbee. You know those evaluations are coming up in two more months."

"I must admit after looking over the weekly reports that Elbee has been sending me, Kim, and the managing partners, he was definitely on point with his assessment. The bigwigs told me that if Elbee can convince as many of the guys to resign as he predicted, both of you will be getting bonuses."

"Why would they give me a bonus? Elbee did all of the work."

"Humph, I can't tell. Your name is on all of the reports."

"He just put my name on the reports. Most times, he was the one in the office working late to verify the information to go along with his reports. All I did was helped him relax and focus when he got frustrated."

"Well, that's what those breasts and hips are for…so you can help the brotha relax. You got 'em from your mama," Carolyn sang as she began to laugh.

"Girl, you're sick, you know that? Although I must say we

do get our workout on. That boy is a freak. It's like he takes Viagra or Cialis as a vitamin, but I don't mind 'cause the sex is great."

"I can't believe what I'm hearing. A few months ago, you told me that you weren't looking forward to having sex with Elbee. Now you're telling me that you and Elbee are having sex on a regular basis and it's great. What the hell happened?"

"Carolyn, that man of mine has gone out of his way to make sure I enjoy sex. He was so good that not only did I have an orgasm, I had *multiple* orgasms. I thought I was about to pass out. Through it all, he was gentle and attentive to all my needs. Something no one else had ever done."

"Ooooh, that's hot. Let me find out my little cousin is getting some on the regular and enjoying it. I know what you're talking about though, because Kim is a freak, too. I guess birds of a feather really do flock together."

The receptionist walked in and interrupted Carolyn and Angel talking.

"Ms. Terry, I wanted to bring you these quality assurance reports before I left for the day."

"Thank you, Tatianna. How did you know they were the reports for the quality assurance?"

"Well, I kinda looked through them. I had to make sure my man, Tyriq, was doing his job. Mr. Nessprin is nice, but I know he's planning on firing some folks around here."

"Bye, girl. I'll see you tomorrow with your nosey self," Angel said, while she, Tatianna, and Carolyn laughed.

"As a matter of fact, I'm leaving, too, Angel. Kim…I mean, Blak said he went to the store and bought some whipped cream and caramel. So, I need a nap before we hook up with y'all for dinner, because after that, it's going to be a long, sticky night."

"I use to be able to say that. Lately, Elbee has either been here late or working with his cousin Benny trying to get the building ready. Then when he does come by early, he's tired because of those dreams he's been having."

"Well, girl, just think. It will all be over soon. The building will be done and the evaluations will be done, too. As for the dreams, you're on your own, but either way, I'm out of here."

"Oh okay, girl. I'll see you later. As a matter of fact, I'm leaving, too."

The Gift

Elbee hurried to the Zales in St. Charles Town Center Mall to pick up Angel's anniversary present. As he parked his car, he realized the commercials he had seen on television really did work. Zales was the first place he thought about when he started looking for some jewelry to give Angel for their anniversary.

Elbee walked up to the counter. "Hello, Ms. Lady, how are you today?"

"I'm fine," she replied.

"I can see that you're fine. What I asked was how you are doing," Elbee responded with a smile that made the sales associate melt.

She began to blush. "I'm doing very well. How can I help you?"

"Is Trey McMichaels in today?" Elbee asked.

"No, he's not in today," she replied.

"Well then, maybe you can help me," he continued.

Speak Now Or...Hold Your Piece

The sales associate leaned in closer to Elbee. "I'm sure I can and in more ways than one. So, tell me what I can do for you."

"Well, aahh," he replied, while looking at her name tag, "Robin, I placed an order about two weeks ago, and I'm here to pick it up."

"Are you sure that's all I can help you with?" Robin asked.

"I don't know. After you see what I'm picking up, you tell me."

Robin went into the back and came out with Elbee's package.

"I see someone has some extremely good taste. What's the occasion?"

"It's our anniversary."

"Isn't that cute," Robin replied sarcastically. "She must be rather special."

"I think she is. I can't speak for anyone else, though."

"Well, let me ring this up for you."

While ringing up the purchase for Elbee, she looked at him with a seductive smile. "So is this all I can help you with?"

"I don't know. What do you have to offer?"

The sales associate tore Elbee's receipt off the register and handed it to him. Then, she handed him one of her business cards.

"My cell phone number is on the card. If you have any jewelry needs or any other needs at all, just call me."

Elbee looked at Robin, licked his lips, and smiled. "I'll be sure to keep that in mind."

"If you lick everything else the way you lick them luscious lips you have, I will wait by the phone for your call."

Elbee grabbed his bag and started towards the door, when

Robin added, "If you call, you won't have to worry about your girlfriend finding out about us. I surely wouldn't want my husband to find out."

Elbee smiled and nodded his head. He couldn't even begin to fathom how easily it was for married people to cheat on their wives and husbands. To him, marriage was sacred, and on that faithful day when he stood in front of God, his family, and friends to proclaim 'til death do us part', he was going to mean it.

Elbee looked down at his watch and realized he needed to get home in fifteen minutes so he could be on time. He had given Angel so much grief about being on time that she was waiting for the day he was late so she could recite his words back to him verbatim.

Guess Who Loves You More

Elbee was on cloud nine when he stepped out the house on his way to pick up Angel. Blak had already left the house, and even though they were going to the same place, they knew they would not end up at the same location at the end of the night.

Dressed in a pair of fresh DeMarco Solar jeans, a button-up shirt with black print, a black, crushed velvet blazer, some black Nike Air Cole Haan shoes, and with just enough Creed cologne, Elbee knew he was looking and smelling good. As he walked to his car, he thought to himself, *If they smell something stinking tonight, it will be me 'cause I'm the shit.*

Elbee got into his burgundy Cadillac Escalade ESV with the gold trim. He knew it was going to be a night to remember. After looking through his CD's, Elbee decided to play *Love Experience* by Raheem DeVaughn. Although he thought the whole CD was hot, he went straight to his favorite song, track three. After the fiasco he had with Tasha, which was the last story, he felt when he finally met that special someone, every time he heard "Guess Who Loves You More" she should immediately come to mind.

As Raheem's voice blasted through the speakers and the words of the song permeated throughout the vehicle, thoughts of Angel began to dance in Elbee's head. He could see all of the different places and settings he had already seen her in, as well as some he hadn't seen her in. He realized not only was she his woman and lover, she was also one of his best friends. Elbee thought to himself, *What more could a man want?*

The two of them did almost everything together. They exercised, rode bikes, went for walks, watched sports, and had some of the most in-depth conversations. Raheem was at the part of the song where he said, "Girl, you are perfect in my eyes," and Elbee began to smile because to him, Angel was perfect. Angel would always complain that she had gained weight, but to Elbee, she was just as sexy now as she was the day they met.

Elbee looked at the present he had bought for Angel, then smiled and thought to himself, *I did good this time. She's going to love this.*

When Elbee pulled up in front of Angel's home, he looked in the mirror to make sure he had it all together. Everyone was going to get a surprise this evening. Elbee had purchased tickets for them to see one of DC's local artists, Sylver Logan Sharp.

Before ringing the doorbell, Elbee braced himself. Although he had been out to a number of shows with Angel, this was their first anniversary together. The first one of a lot more to come he hoped, but he knew fate was a funny thing.

Lady in Public
And Freak in the Bedroom

When Angel opened the door and Elbee looked at her, he was speechless. He had dated a lot of women in his thirty-two years of living, but none he would have considered to be a ten on his scale. There were some sixes, a good number of sevens, a bunch of eights, a few nines, and some damn good twos, but getting a ten was quite a stretch by his standards.

Each man determined where a woman fit on his scale of one to ten differently. Some men judged women solely on their looks, others judged them on their size, some judged them by their personality, and others only considered a woman's financial and social status, but not Elbee. He rated a woman by everything except her financial or social status, and no one quality was more important than the other. One of the qualities Elbee thought he wanted in a woman was for her to be a lady in public and a freak in the bed. He often wondered was that the reason he loved Tasha, because she was a true freak in the bedroom.

Angel wasn't the freak in the bedroom that Tasha was, but her other attributes were so strong they overshadowed that aspect. Angel's honesty about the fact that she never really enjoyed sex when she and Elbee first started dating made Elbee more understanding. It also didn't hurt when Angel went out and bought her own books to read so she could find more ways to please her man.

"Damn, sweetie, you look as good as a ham and cheese sandwich, and you know a brotha loves pork."

"Well, I'm glad you think so. I worked hard to try and impress you," Angel replied.

"If that's what you were trying to do, mission accomplished. All I have to say is that you are one sexy mother...."

"Shut yo mouth!"

"But I'm just talking 'bout Angel," Elbee said, as they began to laugh.

"So you really think I look nice?" she asked, beginning to doubt herself.

"Baby, in the words of Raheem DeVaughn, you are truly perfect in my eyes."

"If I must say so, you are looking rather suave yourself, Mr. Nessprin."

"Well, you know. What can I say?" Elbee joked, while rubbing his moustache, sounding like JJ from *Good Times*. "But, let's get out of here before we're late for our reservations. Plus, you know how Blak acts when he gets hungry. I think that boy is hypoglycemic or something."

"Elbee, we can't go yet. I haven't given you your

anniversary present."

"Can't it wait 'til we get back?"

"No, boy. Open this present."

"Why I gotta keep tellin' you that *boy* is a white racist word!"

Elbee walked over to the table and opened the card that was on top of the box Angel had handed to him. After reading the card, he looked in the box to find season tickets for the Washington Redskins. Elbee gave Angel a hug to let her know how much he appreciated and loved her. When Angel began to pull away so they could leave for dinner, he pulled her back into his arms and gave her a deep, passionate kiss. There was so much love and passion in the kiss that Angel thought she felt her uterus doing flips.

"If we don't leave right now, I don't think we're going to make it to the restaurant for dinner," Angel said, pulling away from Elbee once again.

"You're right, sexy. Because right about now, my soldier is so hard I could cut through diamonds."

"I know. I just need you to be like that later on so you can really show me how much you like your present."

"Girl, you're turning into a lil' freak," Elbee said with a smile.

"I thought that's what you wanted, a lady in public and a freak in the bedroom."

"I do. I just didn't know it would be such an easy transformation."

"It's like a wise old lady once told me. Every woman has some freak in her. It just takes the right man to bring it out."

"Well, I'm glad I was able to help you with that," Elbee

responded.

He then helped Angel put on her coat, and they walked out of the house.

"Your chariot awaits," he stated with a smile as he opened the car door for her.

Angel smiled at Elbee with love and affection, which caused him to feel warm all over. His heart was filled with love for the woman who had repaired his heart when it had been torn apart. He just hoped the present he had for her showed how much he loved her.

Haters

Dinner at Legal Seafood on 7th Street NW in Washington DC was lovely as usual. Everyone was surprised and excited when Elbee pulled out the tickets to see Sylver Logan Sharp at Takoma Station. The venue was known for being a Go-Go spot, but the club owners were starting a new thing where R&B and Jazz artists would perform on Sunday nights. Elbee had picked up Sylver's CD and was blown away with it, so he had to see her in person. So, when he heard she was performing at the Station, he knew he had to be there.

Rhonda was so excited about the evening that she kept calling Elbee to see if he had given Angel her gift. DB and Rhonda weren't able to make dinner due to a previous engagement, so she wanted to know all of the details of the evening and couldn't wait for Elbee to call her.

Elbee had called in some favors. So, when they arrived at the club, they received the VIP treatment. They had a table near the stage with a bottle of Dom Perignon already chilling on it. Cristal may have been the in thing, but Elbee opted for the Dom P because he said it took him back to the days when Rare Essence used to sing about the Dom Perignon Crew at the Go-Go.

The lights went down and saxophonist Brian Lenair began to play a few songs from his album *Journey*, opening up for Sylver. He was definitely a bad boy. His mellow sounds and smooth grooves had everybody in the mood for love. Elbee sat thinking that the promoters couldn't have picked a better person to open up for Sylver.

Brian played for about thirty minutes before ending his set. At that point, Ms. Ressie from WHOLLA, a local radio station, came to the stage and announced there would be a brief intermission before Sylver came on to perform. Elbee sat at the table with the strange feeling that he was being watched. He tried to shrug it off, but the more he tried, the more intense the feeling became. It felt as if someone was burning a hole in his neck with their eyes.

Elbee leaned over and asked, "Blak, is it me or do you feel like we're being watched?"

"El, I think you're being a little paranoid. If we're being watched, it's probably the women watching me since I'm such a fine specimen of a man."

"Dude, Carolyn really needs to get you some help or some prayer. No, scratch that. Yo dumb ass needs both."

Before Blak could respond, the lights went down again and Ms. Ressie came back onto the stage and yelled into the microphone, "Skuwee!"

The crowd responded with loud barks and cheers.

"Is everyone having a good time? Well, now it's time for all of you to get ready for the soulful sounds of Sylver Sharp."

Sylver walked out on stage singing "Don't Give Up". The sister was destined to be one of the hottest artists to hit the scene in a minute. For the next twenty minutes, she sang songs from her newly released CD entitled *Place to Begin.*

It came to a point when Sylver walked to the edge of the stage and said, "Ms. Ressie has informed me that her friend Elbee would like to introduce the next song. Come on up here, Elbee."

It was the moment of truth, and Elbee began to experience a type of nervousness he had never felt before. His stomach immediately balled up in knots, his palms got clammy, and as cool as he thought he was, he began sweating like a Klansman at a Black Panther rally.

Blak, Carolyn, and especially Angel were all stunned. They knew Elbee had clout, but they didn't know that he had this much clout. None of them had a clue as to what was about to happen, but they all were looking at Elbee because they knew he had something up his sleeve. They knew it was just like him to do something wild because he loved to do things big.

Elbee stood up, looked at Angel, swallowed hard, and tried to speak. "Angel, we have been together a year and a half now, and during that time, things were pretty rough. However, you stayed true and faithful to me. So now that times are better for me," he paused and got down on one knee, "I want you to marry me so I can spend the rest of my life telling and showing you how much I love you."

Before Angel could answer, the music to Sylver's song "Lifetime" began to play softly. Elbee was on bended knee before her with a one-carat diamond surrounded by a half carat of baguettes as Angel sat smiling with tears rolling down her face.

"I haven't heard an answer yet!" Blak shouted.

Angel nodded her head and replied yes. At that moment, Sylver began singing the words to a song that seemed to be perfect for the occasion because it described exactly how Elbee felt about Angel.

Blak and Carolyn were congratulating Elbee and Angel on their engagement, when the waiter came over to the table with a bottle of Cristal and a note. The note read: *Congratulations on your engagement. Enjoy it while it lasts because you won't make it to the altar.*

Elbee read the note and frowned. "What the hell is this?"

He called the waiter over to the table to ask who the champagne came from, while he looked around for someone he recognized. When he didn't see anyone he knew, he just balled up the note and mumbled, "Haters."

Tryin' to Get a Number

Sitting on her couch, Deshawn was becoming increasingly frustrated. It had been three months since Rocky asked her to find Angel. She had gone through each and every letter she received from Angel since she had moved. One of them had to give her some insight as to where Angel was living or how she could get in touch with her. She had been through the letters and cards several times with no avail. It was as if she had fallen off the face of the earth. They couldn't have been as close as she thought they were, she reasoned, because if they were, she would know how to contact her.

Deshawn never believed Angel when she would say Rocky was beating her. To her, Rocky could never do anything like that. He was just too kind and too gentle. If he did do something like that to her, she probably deserved it. *I would never give him that reason,* she thought.

Whether or not Rocky abused Angel was not going to be a

concern anymore for Deshawn. Rocky was her man now, and she needed to find Angel to make things official. Since all of the letters, cards, and gifts always had Angel's parents' address on them, she felt it was time to give them a call. She didn't want to call Angel's parents, but she didn't know what else to do. She was getting desperate. She knew she was scheduled to see Rocky soon, and she had to have that info. Deshawn picked up the phone and dialed the number for Angel's parents.

"Hello," the voice on the other end of the phone said.

"Hello, Mr. Terry. How are you today?"

"I could be better, but then again, I could be worse. So, as the song says, I won't complain," he sang. "I know this voice. Is this my baby Deshawn?"

"Yes, sir, it is."

"Well, I'll be. I was just asking Angel about you the other day when she called. How are you, sweetie?"

"I'm fine, Mr. Terry. Just taking it day by day."

"That's all we can do. What can an old man do you for today?"

"I was actually calling to see if you had heard from Angel. I hadn't heard from her in a while, and I was trying to call her, but I misplaced her number."

Deshawn knew if Mr. Terry knew anything he would tell her. She knew Mr. Terry thought the world of her, and he treated her like his own child. There wasn't anything he wouldn't do for his children.

"Deshawn, I sure don't have her number. I don't even know what state my daughter lives in. You know Monica and Angel don't think I can hold water, so they don't tell me much. The only one who knows how to get in contact with Angel is her mother. Hold on for a minute while I get her for you." Mr. Terry put the telephone down and yelled, "Monica, pick up the phone!"

Right on key, Mrs. Terry screamed back, "Who is it?"

"Pick the phone up and see who it is, woman!"

"Don't get smart, Marvin."

Mrs. Terry picked up the phone. "Hello."

"Hello, Mrs. Terry. How are you?"

With an attitude, she replied, "I'm fine. Who am I speaking to?"

"It's Deshawn, Mrs. Terry."

Mrs. Terry didn't like Deshawn, and she never understood why her daughter and husband liked her so much. She always felt that Deshawn was only out for herself. She believed her point was proven when Deshawn broke up with her son the day after he found out he would never play basketball again, but Angel and her father still loved her.

"Hi, Deshawn. How may I help you?"

"Mrs. Terry, I know you don't like me."

"Well, if you know I don't like you, then why are you calling me?"

"I hadn't heard from Angel in a while, so I was wondering if she had sent me any letters. I know she normally sends them through you."

"When was the last time you sent her a letter? Because anything you send her goes through me, too, and I haven't seen anything."

"Mrs. Terry, I don't want to argue with you. I was just trying to get a number for Angel. I had it, but I can't seem to remember what I did with it."

"If you lost her number, all I can tell you is that the next time I talk to her, I will see if I should give it to you. Or you could send her a letter and ask for it. Either way, I won't be giving it to you," Mrs. Terry snapped, then hung up the phone.

Deshawn sat wondering how she was going to get the information she needed. If she didn't have the information Rocky wanted, he was going to be upset with her. She didn't know what to do. Angel could be anywhere. The question was where in the whole wide world she could be. Then the answer hit her: The World Wide Web.

You Play Too Much

"Hello," Elbee answered in a raspy voice. The cell phone ringing woke him up from another restless night. He looked around the house trying to get his bearings and figure out who he was talking to.

"Congratulations," the voice spoke.

"Congratulations for what? Who the hell is this?" Elbee asked, trying to clear the fog in his mind.

The last time Elbee felt the way he did was after a night of hanging out drinking with the guys. He sat up in the bed with his eyes beginning to focus on his surroundings, while the question as to who he was talking to remained unanswered.

"Has it been that long? You used to know my voice well."

"I tell you what. Either you tell me who this is or you can talk to my friend Mr. Click," Elbee snapped.

"This is Tasha, boy."

"Your daddy is a boy. Now what do you want?"

"I see you still take someone calling you *boy* to heart."

"Yes, I do. So, once again, what do you want, Tasha? I don't have time for your games."

"I just wanted to call and say congratulations on your engagement." It was at that moment that her voice turned cold. "Too bad you two won't be getting married."

Elbee snickered. "You play too much. What makes you think we won't be getting married?"

"Because, baby, you know how much I still love you, and I know you still love me. Elbee, I know I hurt you, and I'm sorry. Now it's time for us to get past all of that and get back together," Tasha replied in her tender voice she knew Elbee loved.

"Okay, so what I hear you saying is you're sorry for cheating on me, I should just forgive you, and it will never happen again," Elbee responded.

"Yes, that's what I'm saying. Elbee, we both did things wrong in our relationship, but I forgave you. Now, it's time you stop stringing Angel along so we can get back together. I miss you."

Elbee sat quiet for a moment and then said, "I miss you, too, sweetie. This past year without you has been hard on me. You don't know how many times I picked up the phone to call and ask you could I come back home. I was just scared you would tell me no."

Getting excited to be getting what she wanted, Tasha replied, "Baby, I wouldn't have told you no."

Tasha didn't think getting Elbee back was going to be so easy. Once she saw him propose to Angel at the club, she knew it was now or never for her and Elbee. Tasha knew Elbee was a good man, and she was determined to get him back.

Speak Now Or...Hold Your Piece

"I was afraid Dexter had replaced me in your life. Tasha honey...sweetie...pooh bear...snuggle lumps?"

"Yes, Elbee?"

"I wanna come home, baby."

"You do?" Tasha cooed.

"HELL NO! Did you really think I was going to forget what you did?" Elbee shouted.

"But, Elbee..."

"But my ass. There isn't, nor will there ever again be, an 'us'. Got it? Good," Elbee said, hanging up the phone.

She plays just too damn much, Elbee thought. *I don't know what kind of fool she thinks I am. Wait till I tell Blak about this. Some people are crazy.*

Tasha sat looking at the tape she had just made of her conversation with Elbee. He may not come back to her, but he wasn't going to marry Angel either. Not if she had anything to do with it.

You and Your Women

Elbee was sitting on the living room sofa drinking a Corona and watching *Stomp the Yard*. Just as he was about to enjoy his favorite part when Megan Good was jogging and Columbus Short almost hit her with the riding lawnmower, Blak walked into the house. Elbee and Blak had been missing each other for a couple of weeks. Both had been working late or staying over their respective ladies' homes.

"What up, homie?" Blak spoke as he sat down on the couch with Elbee.

"Just chillin', fool."

"I know you got another one of those cold ones, don't you?"

"Yeah, I got a few more brews," Elbee replied, while handing Blak a Corona.

"Ooh, you watching *Stomp the Yard*. Has Megan done her run yet?"

"Nope, but that's what I'm waiting on."

"I love that part, so I guess I got here just in time."

They sat drinking Coronas and watching the movie, while

taking time throughout to get caught up with what was going on in each other's lives.

"Oh, you know I got things set up so that after everything is done with the reviews, DB and Barron can come on with the company and watch your back," Blak voiced.

"That's cool. I'll have to let them fools know when I talk to them," Elbee replied. "I haven't really talked to them much since I've been working with Benny trying to get my apartment building together."

"How is the building coming along anyway?"

"Everything is going good. We're right on schedule to finish. So, I will be moving real soon."

"Good. Like I told you before that means Carolyn and I can start walking around the house naked."

"You play too much. That was not a good visual. Well, part of it wasn't. Hell, Carolyn is hot."

"Don't make me hurt you."

"I'm just playin', fool. Speaking of playin'. Guess who called me the other day?"

"Who?"

"Tasha's crazy ass."

"What the hell did she want?"

"She heard that Angel and I got engaged, and she thought it was time for me to stop playing with Angel so we could get back together."

"That broad be lunchin'."

"Ya think?"

"Was she serious?"

"As serious as a HIV patient with pneumonia. Then she got mad when I told her that we were never going to get back together."

Blak finished up his beer as the movie was ending. "You and your women. You and your women, dawg," he uttered as he headed off to his room.

Number Change

Angel sat on her sofa trying to unwind. She knew her next day at work was going to be hectic. Elbee had already determined that was when the hammer was going to fall. So, it would be another crazy day.

She started to think about the phone call she received at the end of the day. It bothered her a little bit. Why would somebody call just to see if she would answer? Had Rocky or some of his people found her?

After going over everything in her mind, she came to the conclusion that it couldn't be him. One of her friends told her that the judge had given Rocky a twenty-year prison sentence without parole, and had it not been for one of his flunkies admitting to being the boss he would have gotten a kingpin charge, which carried a life sentence.

Angel started to laugh immediately when she realized he didn't even know where she was living now. As a matter of fact, no one knew where she lived except her parents. Angel was so paranoid that she called all of her girlfriends from her old cell phone so they wouldn't even know her area code.

Angel was so deep in thought that she was startled when she heard the telephone ring. She knew it had to be Elbee checking to see if she had finished the termination letters.

"Hey, babe, what's up?" she said into the phone.

There wasn't a reply.

"Hello, hello. Elbee, can you hear me?"

Not getting a response, she hung up the phone.

"That boy needs to get rid of that raggedy Nextel phone he has," she said to herself.

The phone rang three more times, and each time no one answered. The next time the phone rang, Angel had had enough.

"Why the hell do you keep playing on my fucking phone?" she screamed.

"Girl, what are you talking about, and why are you cursing like a sailor?" the voice asked.

"Who is this?" Angel inquired firmly.

"Angel, this is your mother. What in God's name is going on?"

"Oh, I'm sorry, Ma. Someone has been playing on my phone for the past half hour."

"Playing on your phone? What are you talking about, baby?"

"Someone has been calling me and not saying anything. It's okay, though. I will just have Elbee look into it. Enough about me. How are you and Dad doing?"

"We're fine, sweetie. Your father has started to enjoy his retirement. You know he was about to go crazy when he first retired."

Speak Now Or... Hold Your Piece

"I'm glad Dad is adjusting. I knew if he sat around the house too long he would either go crazy or drive you crazy," Angel said, laughing.

"How is Elbee doing? When are we going to get to meet this young man I keep hearing so much about?"

"Elbee is fine. He just bought a ten-unit apartment building that he's going to renovate and turn into five apartments."

"That's great. Tell him I said congratulations."

Angel was getting ready to tell her mother about the engagement until her mother repeated her question.

"You still didn't tell me when we're going to get to meet him."

"As soon as everything is done with Rocky, I will bring him home so you can meet him. Mom, you and Dad are going to love him. Elbee is one of the sweetest, kindest, most generous, and understanding people I know."

"If he is so understanding and sweet, why do we have to wait until everything is done with Rocky to meet him? He should understand about Rocky," Angel's mother snapped.

"Mom, he doesn't even know about Rocky," Angel replied in a low tone.

"He doesn't know about Rocky! Angel, what's going on?"

"Ma, when I first met Elbee, I told him that I was engaged and we broke up. By the time I realized that I loved him, I was afraid to tell him the truth. Especially since his last relationship ended because his girlfriend lied to him and cheated on him."

"Baby, it's not right to keep your marriage from him. Elbee is going to find out eventually. So, it would be better if you told him now opposed to later. You know it's a tangled web we receive when we try to deceive. Pray on that, sweetie, and I will pray that you do the right thing."

"Yes, ma'am, I will. Now you said Dad was adjusting to his retirement. How is he doing that?"

"He started coaching football at the Boys and Girls Club. He is so excited about coaching that he has already started recruiting players and the season doesn't start until July. But I was calling to find out if you've talked to Deshawn?"

Angel could hear the change in her mother's voice when she asked that question. The sense of dislike in her tone made Angel laugh. She didn't talk to Deshawn as much as she used to since she decided to testify for Rocky. Angel felt that Deshawn should have been more loyal to her than Rocky.

"No, I haven't spoken to her. Is there something I should know about, Ma?"

"Well, your father said I shouldn't say anything to you, but someone broke into the house last week."

"What does that have to do with Deshawn, Ma?"

"She called the house a couple days before the break-in and was asking for your phone number. She told me that she had your number but had lost it, and she was asking me for it. I told her no, point blank."

"Ma, that still doesn't tell me what that has to do with Deshawn."

"Baby, whoever it was that broke into the house only stole my Bible, where I hid a couple dollars, and my address book."

"Please tell me that my phone number and address were not in the book, Ma."

"It was, Angel. I never thought anyone would steal my address book."

"Ma, I asked you to keep my phone number and address

separate from your other addresses for a reason. If I had known you weren't going to do it, I wouldn't have given it to you," Angel said angrily.

"I know, dear. I know."

"Ma, you don't know. If you knew, then you would have done what I asked you to do," Angel said flatly. "I have to go, Ma. Elbee will be here to get me in a few minutes, and I still haven't gotten dressed. I'll call you later."

"Okay, Angel. I love you, sweetie, and I'm sorry."

"I love you, too, Ma."

Angel hung up the phone and tried not to be upset with her mother. Mrs. Terry was sweet, but she could be naive at times. Angel just hoped the prank phone calls and her mother's stolen address book weren't related. Angel didn't think Deshawn would do anything like that, but she could have gotten mixed up with the wrong people. Either way, she was going to call and have her number changed.

I Found That Girl

Deshawn could barely contain the excitement she felt while walking into the prison to see Rocky. She didn't find out where Angel lived, but she found out where Angel worked.

When Rocky walked into the visitor center, Deshawn got upset with the attention Rocky got from the other women in the room. Rocky was always slim and in shape, but since he had been incarcerated, he had buffed up. She could see how his chest poked out and how cut up his arms were.

"Dang, baby, I can definitely tell what you've been doing with your free time," Deshawn said with a smile.

"Well, a brotha gotta do something to help wit' his sexual frustration," Rocky replied as he flexed his muscles.

"When you get out of here, you won't ever have to worry about that again," Deshawn stated, while caressing Rocky's manhood. "Because every time you get Mr. Man here up, I'm going to put him back down."

"I like the sound of that, sexy. Now did you get that package from Tony for me?"

"Yeah, baby, I picked it up. I got something else for you, too."

Rocky signaled for the officer to come take the package from her and then asked, "So what else do you have for me, sexy?"

Deshawn reached back into her purse and pulled out a newspaper clipping with a picture on it.

"What's this?" Rocky queried.

"Look at it," Deshawn begged, smiling. "I found that girl."

Rocky looked at the paper that read *Washington Post* and then at the picture. He began to smile. Could it be? Yes, it was. It was a picture of Angel.

"Is that a picture of Angel?" Rocky asked for clarification.

"Yep, that's her. I couldn't find an address when I was searching for her, so I just googled her name and found this article. I almost didn't find her because she's using her maiden name."

"She's using her maiden name!" Rocky exclaimed. "What the fuck is her problem?"

Rocky looked at the picture again. When he saw a man with his arm around Angel's waist, he lost it.

"Who the fuck is the nigga with his hand on my wife?" he screamed, flipping over tables.

"Why does it matter who he is, honey, if you're planning on divorcing her when you get out of here?" Deshawn snapped.

Rocky looked at Deshawn with fire in his eyes and slapped her. "Don't you ever question me!"

The officers ran over and grabbed Rocky. "Ma'am, your visit is over," one officer asserted as they started to take Rocky to solitary confinement.

Deshawn walked out of the prison crying. Before she could get to her car, a young officer caught up with her.

"Excuse me, ma'am. Are you okay?"

"I'm fine," she insisted, wiping away her tears.

"If you come back inside, I can do the paperwork so you can press charges on the inmate for assault."

"Why would I do that? He was upset and I gave him the attitude. I know he's going through a lot right now, especially with being wrongly convicted. So, I should have been more considerate."

The officer shook his head. He had heard this story before. "I don't care what's going on. He should never put his hands on you. Here's my card in case you change your mind."

Deshawn took the card, got into her car, and pulled off. As soon as she was out of the officer's sight, she threw the card out of the window.

Sparkle

Rocky walked around his cell fuming. Who was the man with his arm around Angel, and why was he touching his wife? He had to get out of prison. He had to claim what was his. As he sat down on his bunk, he remembered what had brought him and Angel together.

Rocky had moved to Georgia to expand the Espanaza drug empire. He had been in town for a month, when he got turned on to the action in town. When he found out who the major players were in town, Rocky's intentions were to kill them and take over their territory, but Ricardo shut that idea down.

"Rock, after all of the years you have been with me, you haven't learned a thing. You don't get loyal soldiers through fear and intimidation. Loyal workers are gained through money and respect. Plus, if you go in and start killing everybody, the police are going to get involved in the wrong way," Ricardo told Rocky.

"What do you mean 'the wrong way', Pops?"

"What I mean is, if you go in and start killing everybody,

you're not going to be able to pay the police to look the other way while we do business. Son, if you want to take over the business someday, you need to know how to be more than just muscle. You have to be brains, as well."

Rocky had learned so much from Ricardo that he made sure he listened when he spoke. Ricardo told Rocky to find an area where no one was working and set up shop. Next, he would put out testers and let everyone know that the price was cheaper than the competition's. Then gradually raise the price once they were hooked and let the runners for the other dealers see how he treated his workers.

As usual, Ricardo was right. When the runners for the other local dealers saw how Rocky treated his runners, they slowly defected to his organization. What amazed Rocky the most was that he was able to take over without anyone getting killed. Since there were no murders, there wasn't any news coverage, and the police on the beat took their payoff and looked the other way.

Things were going fine until Rocky entered the building to his condo and found two of his runners trying to force their way into someone's condo. He realized the condo they were trying to get into was owned by a young lady, and she was screaming for help. Rocky knew if he didn't intervene things could turn out bad. What he didn't need was for two idiots to get arrested for doing something stupid and start dropping names to get lesser charges.

"Yo, fellas, what's going on?" Rocky yelled.

"Ahh hey, Rock, what are you doing here?" one of the runners asked.

"I live in this building. Now don't make me ask you again.

What's going on?" Rocky demanded in a sterner tone.

"Rock, this bitch owes us money," the runner told him.

"First, I need you to watch your mouth and don't ever let me hear you disrespect a woman again. Now, why does she owe you money?" Rocky shot back.

"Her brother sold us a TV that doesn't work, and we want our money back."

"Well, it seems to me that her brother owes you some money, but you two fools are going to barge into her home and do what, get yourselves arrested?" Rocky yelled. "Is her brother a head?"

"Yeah," one of the runners said.

"Then you know when you buy goods from a head, you take a fifty-fifty chance, but what I will do is give you back your money this time. Next time, though, you're on your own, and you let everyone else know that any debts should be collected from the person who owes it and no one else. Do you understand?" Rocky stated harshly so they would get the point.

Angel could barely stand. Her legs felt like wet spaghetti. She thanked Rocky and began to walk over to her couch, when she fell to the floor and began crying. Angel had never been so terrified in all of her life.

Rocky ran over to Angel to make sure she was alright. He was helping her over to the couch, when their eyes met for the first time. Rocky tried to speak, but the words would not come out. Never in his life had he met a woman so beautiful. More importantly, he had seen the sparkle that was in her eyes only one other time in his life. He had seen that sparkle in the eyes of Lillie Mae Barnes, his mother.

Angel looked into Rock's green eyes, then at his smooth,

deep chocolate skin and saw her knight in shining armor. Rocky had come to her rescue when the person who was supposed to be looking out for her had put her in harm's way.

"Are you okay?" Rocky asked.

"Yes, I'm fine," Angel responded.

"I can see that you're fine. I want to know if you're okay," he said and smiled.

Rocky's pearly white teeth gleamed against his dark complexion, and his soft facial expression made Angel want to know about the stranger who had rescued her.

"I'm okay then," she replied with a girlish giggle. "You saved me. How can I ever repay you?"

"You can start by promising me that you will stay away from people like that. Secondly, say you will have dinner with me."

"I would consider it if I knew your name."

"I'm sorry. My name is Rocky Espanaza, but everyone calls me the Rock."

"Your name is Rocky," Angel responded, smiling.

"Yeah, my father was a big Sylvester Stallone fan. He watched every Rocky movie about ten times or so."

"Adrian, we did it!" Angel yelled.

They both laughed at Angel's attempt to be humorous, and then they sat talking for hours. It was the most fun Rocky had ever had with a woman.

Things between Rocky and Angel went on for months. They spent every free moment they had together. There was nothing that Rocky wouldn't do for Angel. There were romantic dinners, trips to exotic islands, and more.

Rocky could not believe he had finally met a woman that he

truly felt comfortable around. With Angel, he understood what his pops was talking about when he said women are either quality or quantity, and to him, Angel was definitely quality.

After dating for eight months, Rocky proposed to Angel, and she immediately said yes. Hoping that Angel would be able to have a calming effect on his son, Ricardo spared no expense on the wedding.

The thought of such fond memories brought Rocky back to reality. He hopped off of his bunk and headed to make a phone call. When Tony heard the recording, he immediately pressed five.

"What's goin' on, Rock?"

"Tony, I got some information for you to check out. I need you to go to Washington DC and check out a company called Beltek Technologies."

"I will get someone on it."

"Tony, I need *you* to go, and I need you to go tonight."

"Man, what's so important that I gotta go tonight?"

"You'll see when you get there and check out that company. Oh and take two guys with you and leave them there. I promise you will understand everything when you get there."

"Aw'ight, man. This shit sounds crazy, but you're the boss, so I'm on it."

"Cool. I gotta go."

"Peace out, Rock. I'll holla."

"I will be with my Angel again," Rocky mumbled to himself as he walked back to his cell.

What a Difference A Year Makes

Angel looked in the mirror and couldn't believe what she saw. She looked terrible after not being able to sleep all night.

"Look at the bags under my eyes. I look rough. I'm glad Elbee didn't come by last night," she told herself.

Hearing that there was a possibility Rocky could be released from prison scared her. Rocky could be one of the nicest people you ever wanted to meet, but he could also be one of the nastiest people and he was very dangerous.

Angel thought back to the first year she and Rocky were together. Everything between them seemed to be perfect. It was as if their relationship was a fairytale.

On day three hundred and sixty-five, though, things started to change. Rocky started staying out all night and becoming paranoid. It seemed as if nothing she did was right. Things came to a head when Angel questioned Rocky about his late hours.

Speak Now Or...Hold Your Piece

"Angel, don't question me," Rocky snarled.

"What do you mean don't question you?"

"Don't make me repeat myself," Rocky said through gritted teeth.

"Rocky, don't talk to me that way!" Angel yelled.

That's when Rocky slapped her, knocking her to the floor.

"I told you not to question me!" Rocky shouted. "Now get your ass in the kitchen and fix me something to eat."

Angel lay on the floor crying. She didn't understand what happened. She didn't know what had changed.

After that day, things only got worse. It seemed that no matter what she did it upset Rocky. Not only was he beating her, he was coming home smelling like other women. Whenever she would try to talk to him, he would get mad and beat her. Then he would buy her expensive gifts to try and make up for what he had done.

She began to feel like a prisoner. Every time she went out, Rocky had all of his runners on the lookout for her. If a man spoke to her while she was out, she would get beat when she got back home. She lost her job because Rocky and his runners were intimidating and assaulting the men that worked with her, although none of them were willing to press charges for fear of retaliation.

Losing her job was the last straw. Angel just couldn't take it anymore, so when Rocky wasn't home one day, she left. Angel was at her girlfriend's house when Rocky showed up and demanded that she come home. When she refused, he busted out all of the windows in her friend's car and slashed her tires. When the friend's fiancé showed up, Rocky threatened to kill him if Angel didn't come home.

Not wanting anyone to get hurt, Angel went back to Rocky. She prayed she would be able to escape his wrath, and her prayers were answered. When she walked into the house, Rocky was sitting on the couch looking at their wedding video with tears in his eyes. She could hear him repeating over and over that he was sorry.

"Rocky," Angel called out to him.

Rocky got up and ran towards her. Angel jumped as he reached out to hug her. The fear in her eyes reminded him of the look he would see in his mother's eyes every time his father came home drunk. Was that who he had become?

"Angel, I'm so sorry. I will change. I will get help. Just don't leave me," Rocky pleaded.

Things started to change for the better after that. Angel remembered getting a receptionist position for Beltek Technologies, and Rocky was no longer abusing her. God had truly answered her prayers or so she thought.

After working at Beltek for a month, the verbal, emotional, and physical abuse began again. Then, it happened...the day when Rocky was lying in wait for Angel to come out of the building. When she came outside talking and laughing with her boss Kim, Rocky attacked him and got himself arrested.

Angel was so deep in thought that she was startled when she heard Elbee calling her name. As soon as he walked through the door to her room, she jumped into his arms.

"Elbee, I love you so much. Promise me that you will always protect me."

He looked Angel in her eyes and kissed her lips. "I won't let anything happen to you. I promise."

I Must Be Outta My Mind

The church was extra crowded for Easter Sunday service. Everyone was at church showing off their Easter outfits. The good Reverend Doctor Leon Lonnie Love presided over the service as usual and preached a riveting sermon on how what you do in the dark will come to the light.

Angel sat in the pews feeling as though Pastor Love's sermon was directed at her. She knew the day would come when she would have to tell Elbee about Rocky and her marriage to him. With the possibility of Rocky getting out of prison soon, she realized that conversation might have to happen sooner than she thought.

Pastor Love had given the benediction and church was dismissed. Blak and Carolyn approached Angel and Elbee to see if they wanted to accompany them to H2O for brunch. DB and Rhonda were going to meet them there.

Angel was a little disappointed when Elbee declined brunch so he could meet Benny and do some work on his apartment building. Elbee was so close to finishing the building that she didn't want to stop his progress. Plus, this would give her a chance to get some advice on what she should do.

Angel gave the man she loved more than anything a kiss. Then, while getting into his SUV, he told her after he finished doing some work on his building that he would pick up some clothes and come spend the evening pampering her.

"Come on, woman. I'm hungry," Blak yelled, laughing.

Angel got into the car in enough time to hear her cousin scolding Blak for teasing her. Angel sat in the backseat listening to *The Greatest* CD by Tigah and trying to figure out how to bring up the subject of her marriage. That was until Blak asked her a question.

"Hey, Angel, do you remember the guy that I beat up the day I hired you as my administrative assistant?"

"Yeah, sort of," Angel answered in a low tone.

"Well, I just got some paperwork from the district attorney in Atlanta saying they might be releasing him."

"Did you know the guy, Angel?" Carolyn asked.

Angel replied yes in a childlike voice. She was still so embarrassed by the events of that day. She had hoped she could divorce Rocky, and no one would be the wiser.

"He's my husband, Rocky," Angel whispered.

"He's your who?" Blak yelled as he swerved to keep from hitting another car.

Blak quickly pulled into the parking lot of Penn Station shopping center. He had some questions he needed answers to, and he couldn't get them while driving without having an accident.

"What do mean your husband? Why am I just hearing about

Speak Now Or...Hold Your Piece

you being married? Better yet, does Elbee know you were married." Blak threw the barrage of questions at Angel.

"No, he doesn't know I'm married," Angel responded meekly.

Blak felt his blood pressure go up ten points as he yelled, "Did you say you're still married?"

Carolyn looked at Angel. She could see the fear on her face and the tears in her eyes. She could feel the pain that her cousin was feeling. Carolyn felt that she had to defuse the situation.

"Kim, please calm down, baby." Carolyn would always call Blak by his birth name when he got too excited. "Let's discuss this like adults. Now, Angel honey, tell us what's going on."

Angel looked at Blak, who had gotten out of the car and started pacing. She immediately began to cry. What could she say to help Blak understand?

"Blak, I'm sorry, but I haven't seen or spoken to Rocky since the day he was arrested," Angel pleaded with him.

"Well, I got two questions for you. If you're so sorry, why are you just saying something now? And why aren't you divorced?"

"Once they searched Rocky's car and found drugs as well as guns, I was too ashamed to say I was married to a drug dealer. Then every time the subject came up, you got so mad that I was scared to tell you."

"But that doesn't explain why you're still married. And what are you gonna do about that ring you have on your finger?"

Angel looked at her finger and broke down. "He beat me, Blak. He beat me. Blak, I followed you here because I was running from him. He told me that he would never let me leave him. He threatened to kill me first. I haven't seen my parents in two years because he has people looking for me."

Unable to bare the emotional stress anymore, Angel dropped to the ground and sobbed uncontrollably. Carolyn held her cousin as tight as she could and tried to comfort her. She, too, was becoming overwhelmed with the grief that Angel was feeling.

Blak walked over to Angel, picked her up off the ground, and gave her a hug. They had been through too much together for him to just leave her hanging.

"Okay, Angel, this is what we're going to do. We're going to take you home and get you straight. Then we will get in contact with my lawyer to get you divorced."

Angel looked Blak in his eyes. "Thank you, but what about Elbee? He's going to be upset when he finds out."

"Let me worry about Elbee. We got history. Plus, I ain't scared of his high-yellow ass," Blak said, laughing.

"Thank you, Blak. I love you," Angel replied, drying her tears.

As they walked back to the car, Carolyn looked at Blak and mouthed, "Thank you. I love you, too."

Blak shook his head and thought, *I must be outta my mind. Elbee is going to lose his mind if he finds this out and then kill us all.*

Method to My Madness

It was a beautiful morning when Angel left home headed to work. The winter had turned to spring, and the leaves could be seen trying to blossom on the trees once again.

She felt refreshed starting another workweek. After not being able to sleep all weekend, she felt at ease once she finished talking to Blak and Carolyn about Rocky on Sunday. Elbee lying next to her on Sunday night definitely helped.

When Angel walked into her office at 9:00 a.m., Tonya handed her a stack of messages. She then informed Angel that there had been quite a few people calling wanting to speak with Elbee. Angel put the messages on her desk and was getting ready to sit down, when the telephone rang.

"Good Morning. Beltek Technologies, this is Angel Terry speaking... No, Mr. Johnson, Elbee is not in the office and he will be out all day... I understand, sir, but he's in class all day and unreachable... Yes, he is checking his messages periodically throughout the day, so he should get the message."

Angel continued receiving calls from Mr. Johnson and some

of the other supervisors all day. She thought it was extremely funny how the thought of their jobs being in jeopardy changed their attitudes towards Elbee and the company's policies.

Shortly after Elbee became the director of the telephony division for Beltek Technologies, Beltek acquired Telecom Technologies. A lot of jobs were going to be spared because of the acquisition, but there was still going to be some casualties. Managers were demoted to supervisors, supervisors to lead technicians, and lead technicians to just plain technicians. There were a lot of people upset about the move until they found out they got to keep their salaries, at least for a little while.

During the acquisition, the management for Beltek was trying to figure out how to cut down on the exuberant severance packages that were proposed. Elbee came up with the idea to have everyone work under him for six months, and after six months, they would all be given an evaluation on their job performance. At that time, anyone whose job performance was low would be terminated. For those six months, the company would take a hit, but Elbee guaranteed it would change after that. Plus, they wouldn't have to pay someone for not doing any work.

Angel remembered that meeting like it was yesterday. She didn't think Elbee's plan would work. She hoped and prayed it didn't blow up in his face. Now that the six months were up, she was starting to realize he had predicted it all.

When she asked Elbee why he was sticking his neck out for the people who had done him wrong, he looked at her and told her that he knew people. Elbee told her that his plan wouldn't let people get something for nothing. All of them would have to work for their dollars. He believed some of them would quit because they had to work for him. The ones that stayed on would have to work to his standards, which would be outlined in the new hire package they would receive and sign for.

Now as Angel sat looking over all of the performance appraisals, she could see that Elbee definitely had a method to his madness. At that moment, she remembered she had some things which needed to be cleared up before Elbee found out.

Angel pulled out the card that Blak had given her and made her call. The lawyer had remembered Blak and really liked him, so he said handling the case would be no problem. Angel informed him that she only had one request, and that was that all of her files have her parents' address in them so she could not be found. Being that she still had bills in her name at her parents' house that wouldn't be a problem.

Angel sat and said a short prayer, asking the Lord to help her get through the mess she was in. After her prayer, she felt a little more relieved. She was getting ready to start typing up the termination letters that Elbee had asked her for, when her telephone rang.

"Beltek Technologies, Angel Terry speaking."

"Just checking," the voice on the other end of the phone replied, then hung up.

Rock-a-bye Baby

"You have a..."

Before the recording could finish, Tony hurried up and pressed the number five to accept the call.

"What up, fool? How you holding up?" Tony asked.

"You know, it's the same fight just a different round, and this week I'm winning," Rocky replied. "Did you check out that info I gave you?"

"Yeah, Rock, I did. That info was right on target. She is living in Maryland. We got pictures of the little birdie going to the grocery store, to church, and to work. She was also hanging out with some guy."

"That's probably her cousin. She used to tell me that she had a cousin who had moved to Maryland that she wanted to visit."

"Well, if that's the case, they're kissing cousins and there's a lot of incest going on in their family."

Rocky sat holding the telephone. His heart had dropped to

his stomach. He never thought she would find someone. They were supposed to be together 'til death.

"Do you know who the muthafucka is?"

"Not yet, but I left the boys there to find out for you, Rock."

"Is my father there?" Rocky yelled. "I need to get out of this hell hole now."

Tony could tell Rocky was upset, and in this state, Rocky talking to his father would be disastrous. If Ricardo found out they were using manpower to follow and watch Angel, heads were going to roll.

"Rock, your pops isn't here. He's in DC right now. But I need you to stay calm, 'cause if your pops finds out we're using manpower to keep tabs on Angel, it might get real ugly around here."

Rocky sat quiet for a second. As much as he didn't want to admit it, he knew Tony was right. He had to keep his cool. Losing his temper was only going to make things worse.

"T, have you talked to Deshawn?"

"Yeah, man. What you tell that broad?"

"I kinda insinuated that once I got outta here we could get married."

"Fool, ain't you already married, and now you're trying to get outta jail to marry that crazy broad?"

"I know, I know. I had to tell her something 'cause you dumb dumbs lost Angel and couldn't find her. So, the only way I could get her to find out the information I needed to locate Angel was if I made Deshawn think we were going to be together when I get outta here."

"So what are you gonna do when you get out? You know that heifer is vindictive. She will tell everything."

"I know that. So, when I get home, we will have one more night together and then rock-a-bye baby."

Tony was laughing when he heard the guys in the background yelling phone check. He knew then it was time to cut the call short. He knew Rock could just go off at any moment, and that would nix his chances of getting out of lockup early.

"Hey, Rock, I'm gonna cut it short, but do me a favor. Stay outta trouble until we can get you out. Your pops has spent a grip to make it happen, and every time you have an issue the DA is pushing your release date back."

"Aw'ight, man, will do. But, Tony, I need you…and I mean *you*…to find out about the guy that Angel has been hanging with."

"Already on it, my brotha. You just keep your head up. You'll be home in a few."

Rocky returned to his cell with Angel on his mind. Who was the man and why was Angel with him? It didn't matter. It would be over once he got home.

Together Everyone Achieves More

Friday morning when Elbee walked through the door of the conference room, all eyes were on him. No one had a clue as to what was about to happen. The rumor was that thirty people had been escorted from the building with their termination paperwork in the past couple days. Everyone was wondering if today was a continuation of the firings.

When the president of the company walked in behind Elbee, people really started getting nervous. Bill Donnelly was a cool, laidback Caucasian whose only bottom line was the dollar. A lot of the technicians thought he was racist and didn't like black people, but that was the furthest thing from the truth. If Bill Donnelly didn't like you, it meant you were costing him money, and he didn't care whether you were white, black, yellow, brown, or red. The only color he saw was green.

"Good morning, guys. I am Bill Donnelly, the man that signs your paycheck. As you all know, there have been some changes made here at Beltek. The changes were made by Elbee, your director of telephony, and approved by myself, Carolyn Terry, and Kim Brown. Elbee will talk to you about all of the changes that are transpiring. I just ask that you all take heed to them or we will make some more," Bill said with a smile.

Mr. Donnelly stepped back from the podium and shook Elbee's hand. He then turned and walked out of the conference room. All eyes immediately shifted to Elbee. If they didn't know before, they knew at that moment that Elbee was working with power.

Elbee began by letting everyone know if they were sitting in the meeting that their job was safe. He also let them know there would be a new chain of command. Deante Barnes would be the manager for the cable division. Ramon Jacobs would be the manager for the telephone division, and Barron Thompson was the new IT person. Then, as promised, the guys that had stuck with him through the rough times of the merger got promoted to leads.

The technicians were glad to see some of their own had gotten promoted throughout the mess that had been called a merger. Elbee had figured by doing some promoting from within, he would be able to get more production from the guys. What came out of it was that the guys saw him as a man of his word.

"As you all have seen, I am not the average supervisor. In the past months, I have reprimanded some of you, laughed and joked with all of you, but most of all, I have gotten down and dirty within the trenches with you. Some of you have called me in the middle of the night, and I came out and completed jobs with you."

Speak Now Or...Hold Your Piece

The technicians could be heard agreeing with what Elbee was saying.

"We are no longer just supervisor and technician. We are a team, and I know there ain't no 'I' in team. Hell, there ain't no 'we' either," Elbee stated as people started to laugh.

Elbee continued. "The best boss I ever had taught me that TEAM is just an acronym that means Together Everyone Achieves More."

One of the technicians yelled out, "Yeah, we all need to stick together and be more comaradic."

Elbee began to laugh as he looked at the technician. "Now, boy, you know that ain't a word."

Still laughing, Elbee ended the meeting so the guys could get to work. Now that he had the staff he wanted, he could be the director that he wanted to be. The way he had set up the power structure, he could take care of other things and not have to worry about anyone wrecking his buffet.

Baby Mama

When Elbee stepped into Jaspers, he immediately felt relaxed. The past four months had been a mental strain as well as a test of wills.

During the day, he was doing everything he had to do so everything ran smooth. In the evenings, he was working on his apartment building with his cousin Benny so he would be able to move in on time. His dreams were still keeping him up at night. Plus, he and Angel were starting to have problems.

Elbee didn't know if it was because he was working so much and wasn't helping with the wedding plans or what. But, Angel had started to seem extremely distant.

"Those Levi jeans fit you real nice," a nice voice said, "but then again they always did look nice on you."

Elbee turned to see one of his childhood girlfriends standing there looking just as good as she did in the tenth grade.

"Are you going to just stand there with your mouth open or are you going to speak?"

"I don't mean to stare, Saundra, but DAMN you look good.

Girl, you're so fine you'll have a brotha going to work on Martin Luther King's birthday."

"Well, thank you," Saundra replied, while turning around to show off her 5'1" toned physique and revealing some nice perky breast, a flat stomach, and nice round buttocks that filled out her size eight Juicy Coutour jeans.

"How have you been, beautiful?"

"I have been good, and yourself?"

"You know, same fight different round."

"I know. So whose daughter are you trying to take home tonight?"

Elbee licked his lips and flashed that smile that made women weak in the knees.

"Now why would you ask me something like that?"

"Because I know you."

"Well, if you must know, I am looking for the fellas. It's just me and the fellas tonight. What are you doing here? I heard you got married to a preacher," Elbee said as he drew a cross across his chest.

"I was, but we got divorced after I found out he was laying more than just hands on some of the women in the congregation."

"WOOOOOOW!"

"Yeah, that's right. Wow."

"So you're out just hanging, huh?"

"Not really. I live near here, so I stopped in to grab something to eat on the way home from our son's basketball game."

"Your son's game? So they're playing Boys Club games on Friday night instead of Saturday mornings now?"

"No, he plays for Suitland, just like you did. Elbee, *our* son is fifteen years old."

"Stop playing, girl. What did you do, get pregnant when I left for the military?"

"Try I got pregnant the night before you left for basic training."

Elbee's mouth got dry and he started to sweat. "But the night before I left for basic training, you were with me."

"I know. Didn't you hear me say OUR son?"

The revelation that he had a son hit Elbee like Roy Jones. His knees buckled, and the only thing that kept him from falling was Blak and DB walking up.

Me Time

Angel grabbed the remote and sat down on the couch. With Elbee hanging out with his boys for the evening, it was going to be a Chinese food and Tyler Perry movies night for Angel. She had *Diary of a Mad Black Woman*, *Madea's Family Reunion*, and *Daddy's Little Girls* stacked on the table for viewing.

"Okay, Angel, what are we going to watch first?" she asked herself.

After a short deliberation, she decided on *Daddy's Little Girls*. She thought Idris Elba was fine. That's why she wanted to watch the movie again. She just didn't like the way Elbee drooled over Gabrielle Union every time he saw her. That's why she had only seen part of the movie.

Angel put the movie into the DVD player and was getting ready to dig into her Hunan Shrimp, when the phone rang. She put her fork down and walked over to the phone.

"I don't know who this is, but if it aint Elbee, they're going to have to call me tomorrow. A sista is like Heather Headley tonight," she said, then started to sing, "I need some me time."

"Hello."

"Hey baby. How are you?"

Angel knew that sweet, soft-spoken voice of her mother's as soon as she heard it. The 800 number she had gotten came in handy when her parents wanted to call her, and that seemed like all the time. She had gotten the number before she left Georgia and then forwarded the calls to Maryland. She was doing her best not to leave a trail so she wouldn't be found.

"Hey, Ma, I'm fine. How are you and Dad?"

"We're doing good, baby. I'm surprised to catch you home tonight."

"Well, Elbee went out with his friends tonight. So, I decided to stay home and have some me time."

"I hear you, girl. Sometimes I wish your father would go out with his friends so I could get some me time. Since he retired, he has been around the house driving me crazy," she said with a laugh.

Giggling, Angel replied, "Ma, you know Dad can't sit still for too long. Hey, I thought he was supposed to be coaching football."

"He is, but it hasn't started yet, and he's like a little child waiting for Christmas."

"Other than getting on your nerves, how is my father doing?"

"He's fine, chile. You know your father. He's trying to get himself into something. So how is my new son-in-law to be? I really would love to meet him before you marry him."

"Ma, please don't start. You know why things are the way they are, but I promise you that they will change soon."

"Okay, baby, but the reason I'm calling you is to let you know I received a disturbing phone call."

"From who, Ma? Was it Deshawn again?" Angel asked, concerned.

"No, it wasn't from that child."

Angel just laughed. She knew her mother could not stand Deshawn, and if she wasn't a Christian woman, it would have been pure hate.

"The call was from the District Attorney's office. They were calling to tell you that Rocky's sentence might be getting overturned on appeal. They wanted to know if you were willing to testify against him."

There was a dead silence on the phone. Angel's chest got so tight it felt like she was having a heart attack. She could barely breathe. *This can't be happening,* she thought. *Rocky was supposed to be incarcerated for at least twenty years. How could this be?*

"Angel? Angel? Are you alright?"

"Yes, ma'am, but I have to go. I'll call you later."

Stayin' for Breakfast

After saying her hellos to DB and Blak, Saundra got her food and prepared to head home. She thought how good it was to see the guys and know that they were still good friends. She looked at Elbee, who was still standing off to the side looking a little shook.

Saundra gave Elbee a hug and handed him her card. "Give me a call this week and we can talk about JR."

"Yeah, yeah. Right, right," Elbee mumbled.

"Bye, guys," Saundra said, waving as she walked out the door.

"Damn, boy, Saundra still phat to death. I can't believe Elbee let that go," Blak stated.

Elbee walked over to the bar, ordered a double shot of Patron, and told the bartender to give the guys whatever they wanted. Saundra had dropped a hell of a bombshell. *How is this going to play out?* Elbee thought. *Better yet, what is Angel going to think?*

"Man, Saundra still got you shook after all these years,"

Blak chuckled, drinking his drink.

"Did you see how she was looking in them damn jeans? I can understand why my boy is still a little shook behind her," DB added.

"Yeah, but that's not what has me shook," Elbee admitted.

"Then what is it, fool?" DB questioned.

Before Elbee could answer, Ramon stepped up to the bar. "Man, y'all are not going to believe what happened to me last night."

"And what up to you, too, fool," Blak admonished.

"What's going on, fellas?" Ramon said, while motioning the bartender over to them. "The next round is on me," he continued.

"We know," DB replied.

Elbee was still dealing with the news he had just received as he sat listening to his buddies go back and forth with verbal jabs. It was funny, but for as long as they had known one another that was their way of dealing with each other.

Ramon got his drink and took over the conversation. "Do any of you remember me telling you about this sexy little thing I met from Baltimore?"

"You mean Baby Gold Mouth?" Blak interjected, laughing.

"She ain't got no gold in her mouth, but whatever. She called me last night and asked me about coming to get close and watch some movies. So, I say okay and hit the road headed to B-more. I'm halfway there, when I get a call asking would I stop and pick up some barnyard pimp."

"Pick up some what? Some barnyard pimp? What the hell is that?" DB exclaimed.

"Barnyard pimp, fool! You know, the poor man's steak,"

Ramon answered.

DB was still looking confused about what Ramon was talking about.

"Chicken, fool, chicken!'" Ramon snapped.

"Nigga, you're the most countrified Panamanian I have ever met. Go on with your story," Blak said, laughing.

"So she asked me to stop and get some CHICKEN," Ramon emphasized, "because her girlfriend had stopped by and they were hungry. I'm thinking, 'aww sookie sookie now, a threesome'," Ramon explained.

"Yeah, you would, you slut bucket," Elbee interjected.

"Slut bucket? Wow! That's deep coming from the guy who had a threesome with two lesbians," Blak quipped.

"Hey, I didn't hear about that one," DB joked.

"We're not talking about me. This is all about Ramon. Go ahead, Ramon," Elbee insisted.

"Now I get to ole girl's house. We're chillin' watching the movie and having a good time. The girlfriend leaves, so my chances of a threesome go out the window, but I'm thinking that's cool. After her girl leaves, though, she tells me that she's going to bed and I should sleep on the couch until the next morning. Then she gave me the 'I'm gonna fuck the shit outta you' smile," Ramon alleged.

"What the hell? Have any of y'all ever got that smile before?" Blak joked.

"Not me," Elbee answered.

"I think my meter reader gave it to me before. Then I got a high-ass water bill," DB added, cracking up.

The bartender brought over some more drinks, while Ramon continued. "Whatever! You niggas know what I'm talking

Speak Now Or...Hold Your Piece

about. Anyway, I'm laying on the couch half sleep, waiting for my time to get me some goodies. Then about six in the morning, I hear some keys at the door and some guy came walking up in the house."

"Let me find out you were about to get your ass whooped, Ramon," DB interrupted.

"I thought it was her brother or her cousin. That was until dude went into her room and came out with just his boxers on. Then she came out of the room acting all nervous and telling me I had to leave."

Everybody was laughing, including the bartender that had been eavesdropping on the conversation.

"To add insult to injury, the bama was in the kitchen and waited until I got to the door before saying, 'You not staying for breakfast?' I wanted to punch him right in that gold tooth he had in his mouth," Ramon hissed.

Elbee almost fell off his barstool he was laughing so hard. DB and Blak were both laughing so hard that they were literally crying.

The bartender walked away and came back with four drinks. "Man, I'm sorry about ear hustling, but that was the funniest damn thing I've ever heard. These drinks are on me. You made my night."

Ramon looked at everyone still laughing at his expense, drank his drink, and said, "Fuck y'all. I'm going home."

"Aww, Ramon, don't act like that!" DB hollered, still laughing.

Ramon shot him the bird and walked out the door.

Snitches Get Stitches

Elbee couldn't believe his eyes when he pulled up in front of his building. There was glass all in the driveway, trash on the lawn, and the windows in the bottom units had been busted out. He sat in his truck wondering how he was going to have a nice place with trifling people hanging out in the neighborhood. Cleaning up the neighborhood was going to be harder than he thought.

Ramon and DB pulled up shortly after Elbee got out of his truck.

"What the hell happened, Elbee? Did you have a party and not invite a brotha?" Blak asked, laughing.

"Man, that shit ain't funny. I'm spending too much damn money for people to be messing up my property. That's alright, though. I got something for these ghetto bastards around here. I'm definitely going to change the game up on them," Elbee replied with anger in his voice.

"Yeah, yeah, yeah. Stop trippin' and let's just clean the

mess up," DB responded.

Three little boys rode their bikes up and asked, "Aren't you Deante' Barnes, the guy that played defensive back for the Terrapins?"

"Yep, that's me, little man. What you know about me? You're too young to know anything about any of my football feats."

"My father said he went to school with you when y'all went to Suitland, and he talks about you all the time. Saying how if you hadn't blown out your knee, you would have been the best cornerback in the NFL."

"Your pops is a smart brotha, lil' man."

"Hey, if we clean your yard up, will you pay us?" the little boy asked.

Elbee looked at the boy who appeared to be the oldest. "I'll give each of you twenty dollars if y'all do a good job. Hey, did any of you happen to see who did this?"

All of the little boys said no except one. He dropped his head and could barely look Elbee in the face.

"If you know something, little man, you can tell me. I got your back."

One of the other little boys spoke up. "We ain't no snitches."

Ramon started laughing when he heard the little boy say that. It amazed him how confused the children of today were. To think saying something about someone messing up your neighborhood was snitching. He remembered making sure no one came through and messed up their neighborhood when they were young. If you didn't live in the neighborhood, when you came through, you had to respect everyone and everything in the hood or else suffer the consequences from the neighborhood dudes.

"Listen up, fellas. Telling on someone who is messing up your neighborhood is not snitching. That's called protecting your way of life. Now, if you and your man steal something from the 7-Eleven and you get caught, you telling on your man is snitching."

"But the rappers in the videos keep saying if you talk to the police or tell someone if you saw something that you're a snitch and snitches get stitches," the little boy replied.

Elbee walked over to the youngster. "Do you love your mother and father?"

The little boy nodded his head yes.

"Okay, then. If someone hurt one of them and the police didn't know who did it, wouldn't you want me to tell them if I saw who did it?"

"Yes."

"Well, that's how I feel now. I paid a lot of money for this building, and I'm paying a lot of money to have it fixed up. So, I don't want anyone messing up something I'm spending a rack of money on."

All of the boys chimed in, "Yes, sir."

"That's cool, fellas. By the way, my name is Elbee. That dude over there is Ramon, and apparently y'all already know who DB is."

The oldest looking boy replied, "I'm Lil' Tim." He then pointed at the other two boys. "That's Kennedy, and that's my brother Tyren with the runny nose."

"Alright, Lil' Tim, I got a deal for you and your buddies."

"What's the deal?" Kennedy asked, excited.

Speak Now Or...Hold Your Piece

"Once all the work is completed and all of the tenants move in, I will pay each of you fifty dollars every two weeks for helping me keep the building and the grounds clean."

The boys were saying yeah, slapping hands, and giving each other five. They were excited about being able to make a little money.

"To finalize the deal," Elbee said, "I need to speak with your parents to make sure it will be okay with them."

"What about their grades?" DB interjected.

"Oh yeah, for every grade you get below a C, I'm going to dock your pay five dollars. Is that cool?" Elbee cautioned.

"Awww man," Tyren whined, "that means I gotta do my homework."

"Yeah, you gotta do your homework, little man. Alright, boys, get to work," Elbee said, laughing.

"Elbee," Kennedy spoke up, "I saw the people that trashed your yard."

"Do you know the guys, Kennedy?"

"Nope. I don't think they were from around here. I know they weren't from the neighborhood."

"How do you know that?" Ramon interjected.

"The tags on their truck had a peach on it, and them bamas had gold teeth in their mouths. You know we don't do that shit around here."

Elbee, DB, and Ramon started laughing at Kennedy's deductive reasoning.

"Okay, we got you, but don't be cursing, lil' man," DB told him.

"Fellas, can y'all help me clean this mess up? I got a hot date with Angel for our anniversary."

127

"Yeah, we'll help, but you owe us big for this one," DB said.

Elbee was turning to go into the apartment building to see if anything else had been damaged, when two gentlemen walked up. Elbee had the funny feeling that he had seen one of the guys somewhere before, but he wasn't sure if he really had. The one guy that Elbee thought he recognized walked up to him while the other stranger stayed at the edge of the driveway.

"Excuse me, homie. Which one of you fellas is Elbee?" the stranger asked.

All of the guys started moving towards where Elbee was standing. The two strangers hadn't noticed Ramon and DB when they walked up.

"Who's asking?" DB and Elbee asked in unison.

"A friend," the stranger remarked.

"We don't know you, partner," Ramon snapped.

The stranger looked at Elbee, and then with a sinister grin, he said, "You will."

With that, the stranger abruptly turned and walked away as he mumbled, "Another time, another day."

Taking out his cell phone, Elbee began to dial a number.

"Is everything alright, Mr. Elbee?" Tyren asked.

"Everything is cool, Shorty Doo Wop. Go ahead and get to work so I can talk to your parents about our deal."

The phone rang twice.

"Talk," the voice bellowed.

"I got a problem."

Georgia on My Mind

Angel watched as Elbee sat playing in his plate of Alfredo. She had never seen him so preoccupied before. Even when his neck was on the line for the performance appraisals at work, he never seemed bothered.

"The job announcement for the new technicians was posted today," Angel said, trying to make conversation.

"Okay," Elbee replied without looking up from his plate.

"We posted it on the site for handicapped people."

"That's cool," he replied.

"Oh yeah and I had sex with three of the technicians today," she said, trying to get a rise out of him.

"That's good," he said.

"Elbee, what's going on with you?" Angel queried, but received no response. "Elbee!" she yelled, slamming her hand on the table.

Elbee looked up from his plate. "Why are you yelling, sweetie?"

"Why am I yelling? I'm yelling because I have been talking to you for the past ten minutes, and you haven't heard a word I said."

"I'm sorry, baby girl. I've had something that I've been dealing with for a couple of days, but you have my undivided attention now. So what's up?"

"You tell me what's up. You've seemed out of it ever since you and the guys were over at the apartment building the other day."

Elbee sat at the table thinking about that day. The sinister smile the stranger had on his face had given him an eerie feeling. Who were these guys and what did they want?

"So what's going on, Elbee?" Angel asked.

"Nothing you need to worry about. I got it all under control."

"What is it you have under control, sweetie?"

"Well, if you must know, I had some words with a couple of guys at the apartment."

"Are they guys from the neighborhood looking to cause trouble?"

"Naw, they're from out of town from what one of the little kids in the neighborhood told me. I think them bamas are from Georgia."

Hearing Elbee say they were from Georgia made Angel extremely nervous. *Could they be guys that work for Rocky? They couldn't be. No one even knows where I am, not even my parents,* she thought. She had to talk to Mr. Feinstein and figure out what was going on with her divorce.

Trying to shake the feeling he was having, Elbee attempted to finish his food.

"Hey, which three technicians did you have sex with? 'Cause I'm gonna dock their pay."

Angel walked over and sat in Elbee's lap. "Boy, you're crazy."

"Yeah, yeah, but I'm crazy for you," he responded, kissing Angel on her neck and caressing her sweet spot. "Umm, no panties on, just the way I like you."

Moral Turpitude

Angel had tossed and turned all night long after talking with Elbee. She was hoping or more so praying that what she thought was happening wasn't happening. She couldn't wait to talk to her lawyer. If Elbee found out about Rocky before the divorce was final, things could get disastrous.

Angel got out of bed, showered, and dressed quickly. She wanted to get to work early enough to talk to Kim and Attorney Mr. Feinstein before anyone got into the office.

She looked at Elbee sleeping peacefully. Normally, she would have wakened him up so he could get ready for work, but she decided against it since he hadn't been getting much sleep lately. She knew he had to be extremely tired because he usually would wake her up for some playtime when she fell asleep during a massage, but this morning, he was still resting.

The ride from Fort Washington to the Beltek offices in Lanham seemed much longer. The people on the road seemed to be driving a little more aggressive than usual. *Or am I just in a hurry to try and get some answers?* she thought.

Angel pulled into her parking space, parked her car, and hurried into her office. She sat down at her desk and picked up the telephone to call Mr. Feinstein. She had dialed the number and the phone was ringing, when she looked at the clock and realized it was only 7:50 a.m. She would have to wait at least ten more minutes.

Most law offices didn't open until 9:00 a.m., but not Feinstein and Associates. You could count on them taking their first call at 8:00 a.m. Donald Feinstein had followed in his father's footsteps and became a lawyer. He was an excellent lawyer, but what made him stand out from the rest of the lawyers in the firm was that he was a black Jew. His father was white and his mother was black, so he learned growing up that his name would get him in the door but having superior skills and knowledge would keep him there. That's why when he started his own firm, he decided to open his offices at eight o'clock rather than nine.

The phone had rung five times and Angel was getting ready to hang up, when someone answered.

"Feinstein and Associates. Donald Feinstein speaking."

Angel blew a sigh of relief. "Good morning, Mr. Feinstein. How are you this morning? This is Angel Terry."

"I am doing great, Ms. Terry. How are you this fine morning?"

"I am blessed and highly favored."

"How can I help you, Ms. Terry?"

"I know it has only been a couple of weeks since I contacted you, but I was wondering how things were going with my divorce."

"Well, Ms. Terry, I have some good news and I have some

bad news. Which one would you like first?"

"Angel took a deep breath and sighed. "Give me the bad news first."

"The bad news is I found out you lied to me."

"What do you mean lied to you?" Angel repeated nervously.

"Ms. Terry, I found out that you do know where your husband is and you know how to get in touch with him."

Angel sat on the other end of the phone speechless. How did he find out where Rocky was? She was sure she hadn't given him enough information to actually find him. What was she going to do now? Rocky would surely contest the divorce.

Feeling Angel's disappointment, Mr. Feinstein decided to let her off the hook.

"As I told you, Ms. Terry, when I take on a client, I do my best to find out everything I can about them so I never get surprised in court and they hang themselves. Had I not checked on you, you would have gone to court and perjured yourself, giving your husband every right to challenge the divorce. Now that I have said all of that, do you want to hear the good news?"

Feeling like a little child being scolded, Angel replied, "Yes."

"I just saved a bunch of money by switching to Geico."

They both laughed.

"Seriously, instead of filing your divorce on the basis of desertion, I filed it on the grounds of moral turpitude."

"I'm lost. What does that mean?"

"That means that since your husband was sentenced to twenty-five years in prison, you are eligible for divorce and he can't contest it. So, since you gave me power of attorney in this matter, guess what?"

Speak Now Or...Hold Your Piece

The suspense of knowing what was going to happen was killing her. "Please just tell me, Mr. Feinstein."

"Ms. Terry, as of 5:00 p.m. yesterday you are officially divorced. I must let you know, though, that during my investigation I found out that due to irregularities in your ex-husband's case he might be getting released soon."

"Mr. Feinstein, did I hear you say that Rocky could be getting out of prison soon?"

"Yes, Mr. Espananza could be getting out soon. When I learned of that information, I went back to the judge that granted the divorce and asked for a restraining order. When he read over what he was charged with, along with the fact that you wouldn't testify for him, the judge granted the order."

"Thank you, Mr. Feinstein. You just don't know how much your work has been appreciated."

"Well, Ms. Terry, you can show your appreciation by sending me your final payment," Mr. Feinstein said, laughing.

"I'm writing your check as we speak. You should receive it in a few days. Once again, thank you."

Angel leaned back in her chair, feeling like the weight of the world had been lifted off of her shoulders. Now she could confess that she had been married before. Elbee wouldn't feel like she lied to him because he had never asked had she been married. Just as she started to get comfortable, her office door opened.

"How are things with Mr. Feinstein going?" Blak asked with a look of concern on his face.

"I just spoke with him. The divorce is final as of yesterday."

"That's good because your ex-husband will be out in two weeks."

Til Death

"Espananza, you got mail!" the officer yelled.

Rocky got off his bunk and made his way to the guard's desk. He had been in prison for one year, eight months, three weeks, and two days. This was starting to become monotonous to him. He was tired of people telling him when to eat, when to work out, and when to sleep. This was not his idea of living, and he was becoming more and more frustrated. He felt he should have been home by now, but his father had been too busy traveling to handle the business of getting him free.

The new correctional officer looked at Rocky strangely when he stepped up to the desk. "I called Espananza, convict, and your black ass don't look Hispanic."

"Whatever, man, just give me my fuckin' mail."

"I don't have mail for your black ass. I got mail for an Espananza."

Rocky was already frustrated from being in prison for so long, and this new guard was starting to make things worse.

Speak Now Or...Hold Your Piece

"Look, man, give me my damn mail and I won't have to fuck you up. I'm really not in the mood to play with your ass today."

The guard started making his way from around the guard's desk so he could deal with Rocky, when a senior officer showed up. He was going to let the new officer start making a name for himself with the prisoners until he realized he was trying to make his name off of Rocky, and that really wouldn't have been a good thing.

"Johnson, what's the problem here?" the senior officer questioned.

"I called for Espananza, and this convict showed up and started talking smack."

"Well, he showed up because he is Rocky Espananza. So, just give him what you have for him and let him go back to his cell."

"Yeah, Johnson, give me what you have for me and let me go back to my cell." Staring at the young officer with disdain, Rocky snatched his mail. "Ya ignorant bastard."

"Keep talking and watch what I do," the officer replied.

"Nigga, you aint gonna do shit. I promise you if you try something, your family will regret it," Rocky interjected before turning to walk away.

The officer started to walk towards Rocky, when the senior officer grabbed him and began explaining to him who Rocky was. There was no need for him to put his family in jeopardy over some dumb stuff.

Rocky got to his cell and looked over the letters he had received. One was from his lawyer and the other was from the court. He opened the letter from the lawyer and started to jump for joy. This was the letter he had been waiting for. It outlined the conditions of his release and his release date.

The next letter sent him into a rage, though. He could not believe what the papers were saying to him. As he sat and read the legal documents, he realized these documents were informing him that he and Angel were divorced. They also detailed the restraining order she had been granted.

Rocky was so furious that he went straight to the phones to call Tony. He needed him to be ready, because when he got out of prison, he was going to kill anyone that came between him and Angel.

The usual recording preceded Tony pressing five to accept the call that he knew was from Rocky.

"What up, Rock? You out in a few weeks, homie."

"Yeah, I know. I got the paperwork, but I also got paperwork saying that I was divorced and have to stay away from Angel. Did you or Pop know about this shit?"

"Naw, dawg. If I knew about it, I would have told you. How can she get a divorce without you knowing about it?"

"Man, I don't know. This damn paperwork says something about moral turpitude. I don't even know what the hell that is."

"Do you want me to have the lawyer look into it?"

"Yeah, do that, and make sure this shit is legal. Have you and the boys been keeping an eye on Angel and her little friend?"

"Sure have. Do you want them to reach out and touch somebody?"

"Yeah, yeah, do that. Not her, though, but let him feel the pain a few times. Then I'll speak to him personally when I get out."

Speak Now Or...Hold Your Piece

"I got you, Rock."

Rocky ended his call with Tony and went back to his cell. Angel was crazy if she thought she was going to leave him. He would kill her before he let that happen. Til death do us part is what he said when they got married, and that's what he meant.

Dana Don't Lie

Pacing the living room floor of DB and Rhonda's Waldorf home, Elbee didn't know where to begin. He had been dealing with the bombshell that Saundra had dropped on him on his own for a couple of weeks. He needed to talk to someone that he knew he could trust to keep his secret. More importantly, he wanted someone that he knew would not judge him.

DB and Rhonda sat on the couch watching Elbee literally try and walk a hole into their newly purchased Persian rug. They knew that whatever the problem was, it had to be serious. Out of all the years they had known him, they had never seen him this rattled. That was the reason he was the rock in their inner circle, because he was always calm under pressure.

DB couldn't take it anymore. "What's up, El? Is everything alright?"

"Man, I got issues," Elbee whined.

"We know you got issues. You've had issues ever since we've known you. So what's wrong?" Rhonda replied, laughing.

"This is not a laughing matter, Rhonda!" Elbee exclaimed. "I have real issues. I mean issues that could keep me from getting married."

"Elbee, you didn't cheat on Angel, did you?" Rhonda shouted.

"Who is she, dawg? What does she look like? Does she have big breastsisis like casaba melons?" DB interjected.

Elbee shook his head in disbelief. "No, Rhonda, I haven't cheated on Angel, and your husband is an idiot. Plus, why couldn't I have found out that she was cheating on me?"

"Because we know your track record with women," Rhonda answered. "So now, if you cheating is not the problem, then what is it?"

"Well, as DB already knows, I ran into Saundra Thompson a.k.a. Saundra James, with James being her married name, a few weeks ago."

"Oh, you did? How is she doing?" Rhonda asked.

"She's fine. My goodness, she is fine," Elbee repeated.

"See that comment right there? That's why you get accused of cheating," Rhonda remarked.

"Well, when we were talking, Saundra told me that she is recently divorced and has a fifteen-year-old son named Elbee Elton Thompson."

There was a hush over Jerusalem. It was as if the name connection hit Rhonda and DB at the same time. They both had a look of confusion on their faces.

"Isn't your name Elbee Elton?" DB asked in amazement.

"Yes, it is. Give that man a cookie."

"What are you saying, Elbee?" Rhonda quipped.

"What I'm saying, Rhonda, is that I have a son."
"How did... Better yet, when did all of this come about?" DB babbled.
"We spent the night together before I left for basic training and she got pregnant."
"Are you sure the boy is yours?" Rhonda questioned, sounding concerned.
"Yep, he's my son. I know because Dana told me so, and Dana don't lie."
"Who the hell is Dana, and how can you be so sure she ain't lying?" DB exclaimed.
"Dana. You know D-N-A," Elbee responded, laughing.
"Alright, Madea," Rhonda replied. "So if she knew you were the boy's father, why is she just telling you?"
"That's what I don't know, Rhonda, but I'm going to find out. My dilemma, though, is when should I tell Angel?"

No Easy Win

Chuck Brown had everyone in the club partying like rock stars. The smooth tones of the band's go-go beats and Chuck's signature baritone vocals always seemed to have that effect on his followers.

Elbee was standing by the bar just hanging out. He had taken a rare night off from working on his apartment building and decided to stop by the Classics Nightclub to hear some music and have a drink, which he so desperately needed. He still was trying to figure out how he was going to tell Angel that he had a son. The night was going pretty good until some guy bumped into him and spilled his drink all over Elbee's cashmere sweater.

"Damn, dude, you just gonna spill your drink all over me and keep on moving," Elbee said, wiping his sweater off with a napkin.

"Fuck you and your clothes, you red nigga," the guy replied.

"Fuck me! Fuck me! Slim, you must be outta your rabbit-ass mind!" Elbee snapped, trying not to be too upset.

Elbee could not believe the idiot had just messed up a hundred and fifty dollar cashmere sweater and then wanted to be all huffy. He was definitely not in the mood for the nonsense. Not tonight.

"Look, man, roll on," Elbee uttered, shaking his head.

Elbee finished his drink and began making his way towards the exit. He was no longer in the mood to get his groove on. Since it was still early, he decided to call Angel to see if he could still get some snuggle time in. Even that idea was short lived.

"Aww, is the wittle baby leaving 'cause him shirt got all messed up," the guy said, as if he were talking to a little baby.

Elbee snickered. "Slim, you better go 'head with that bullshit. 'Cause the way I'm feeling right now I'm sure to beat that ass and quick."

Elbee began removing the soiled sweater he was wearing. It was then that the drunk realized Elbee was a lot bigger than he looked in clothes. That didn't deter him from his quest, though. He was determined to make a name for himself.

Someone told a few people about the ruckus that was taking place outside of the club, so a crowd had began to form. Elbee and his cousins had made a name and a reputation for themselves, so hearing that he was outside being harassed had people wanting to see what was going to happen.

"So I see you gonna keep on walking, huh? I knew your punk ass was soft. Everybody is always talking about how tough Elbee Nessprin is supposed to be, and here you are whining over a shirt. You's a bitch!"

Oohs and aahs started coming from the spectators that had gathered around. As much as Elbee wanted to walk away, he knew that wasn't an option. His reputation and his manhood were both on the line.

When Elbee turned and walked towards the stranger, he quickly realized it was the guy from that day at his apartment.

"Slim, you don't fuckin' know me. So, I suggest you walk away, young buck, because this ass whippin' ain't worth it."

"You suggest I walk away," the stranger mocked with a nerdy white boy tone. "Fuck you, nigga," he continued, then threw a punch with all his might that connected with Elbee's jaw.

Elbee stood looking at the stranger with a look of confusion on his face. The punch did not even faze him. People in the crowd could be heard saying, "Run, boy, run!" The young man also began to think the money that he got paid might not be worth it.

Elbee looked at the stranger. "First, I wanna know why you hit me. Next, I wanna know why you didn't knock me out."

At that point, Elbee hit the guy with a barrage of punches, knocking him to the ground. He was about to start stomping him, when a bouncer from the club grabbed him.

"Elbee, what's going on? We don't need this type of trouble here," the bouncer scolded.

"That boy punched me in my face. What was I supposed to do?"

"Alright, man, but I need you to get outta here. The police are on the way."

"Good looking out. I'll take care of you later."

Elbee got into his SUV and left the scene. The police arrived, flying into the parking lot just as he made the right turn onto Allentown Road. Hard as he tried, he could not figure out what was on that boy's mind.

In the back corner of the Classics parking lot, Tony and one of his workers sat observing everything that had just happened.

The worker looked at Tony. "He's not going to be intimidated easily."

"I see. That dude definitely ain't no easy win. I don't think Rock can handle him. We just gonna have to put some hot ones in him."

Seventeen

Thursday evening and it had been a hellacious day. Elbee had every intention of going to Blak's house and going to bed when he got off work, but his mother had called and made him promise to come by her house. He didn't know what the big deal was, but Barbara Jean Nessprin wasn't the type of person that took no for an answer when she wanted something. He thought about just going home anyway, but he knew his mother would have his head if he didn't stop by there.

When Elbee pulled up in front of his mother's home, he began to wonder what was going on. He saw all of the cars of his aunts and uncles in front of the house. Benny's car was even parked out front. It wasn't his mother's birthday because it was a few days before the wedding this year. *Somebody must have died,* he thought.

Elbee walked into the house to what seemed like a party. *It can't be anyone's birthday,* he kept telling himself. He had everyone's birthday in his phone so he wouldn't forget.

Therefore, his phone should have alerted him.

As he walked through the house looking for his mother, Elbee saw his favorite aunt, Dee-Dee. She was his mother's older sister and she, along with her husband Tru, had graciously taken them in when his mother had left the man that he thought was his father for years. He found out he was his stepfather when he graduated from high school.

"Hey, Auntie," Elbee said, giving her a hug and a kiss on the cheek. "How are you doing?"

"I'm fine, baby. Thank you for hiring your cousin to renovate your building for you. He was able to get a lot more contracts after they saw what he did with your building."

"Auntie, you don't have to thank me for that. That's what family is for, and your husband, my favorite uncle, taught me that," Elbee said, smiling because he made his aunt proud. "Do you know where my mother is hiding?"

Aunt Dee-Dee pointed towards the kitchen where Elbee could see his mother sitting at the table talking to someone. Elbee made his way through the crowd of people while saying hi to his cousins and family friends. When he got to the kitchen, he saw a face that he remembered vaguely from pictures. The face had aged some, but it was still strong and good looking. What was strange to him was that the man's face looked just like his face.

The man sitting next to his mother stood, looked him in the eyes, and smiled. "What's up, boy? You ain't got no love for your blood?"

"What's going on, man? How have you been?"

"I've been good, man. Look at you, though. You're not the scrawny little boy I left seventeen years ago. Just one question,

Speak Now Or...Hold Your Piece

though. Are people still chasing you home from school and taking your lunch money?"

Elbee snickered. "Naw. Fortunately for me, after my mother left the abusive man that I thought was my father, who coincidently used to beat my ass for nothing, my uncle Tru—God rest his soul—and Benny made sure that changed."

Benny jumped in to ease the tension. "Uncle Ricky, you know I couldn't have people beating up my little cousin. So, I taught him how to handle his business."

"That's good, Benny. I believe you did a good job looking out for your cousin."

Elbee walked over to his mother and gave her a kiss on the cheek. "Mom, if he's the reason you called me over, I gotta go. I have a lot of work to do tomorrow. So I will call you later."

"Elbee, we need to talk," Ricky stated firmly.

"And we will in about seventeen years."

Play Me

Angel was in a great mood. Not only was it a beautiful day in May, but she had just picked up her wedding gown. Her parents had called, and they were coming to town for a visit. To her, everything was as good as could be when she walked into the office.

"Hey, Tatianna girl. What's going on?" Angel asked, sounding cheerful.

"What are you all happy about?" Tatianna replied.

"Well, I just talked to my parents, and they're coming to town for my wedding. Plus, I just picked up my wedding dress. I'm going to be a bride."

"Oooh, let me see your dress. I wanna see it."

Tatianna followed Angel into her office so she could see Angel's dress. As they walked through the door of her office, Angel noticed there was a small package on her desk.

After showing Tatianna her dress and chitchatting about the colors of the wedding for twenty to thirty minutes, Angel turned her attention to the package that was on her desk. She looked at the package, and when she noticed it didn't have a return address, she got nervous. *Who would be sending me a package?* she asked herself. *This package could have anthrax in it for all I know.*

Sitting down at her desk, Angel picked the package up and shook it. *Why would anyone be sending me some damn anthrax?* she said, laughing to herself. She opened the large envelope to find a CD and a note that read: *Play me.* After looking at the note that was simply signed *from a friend,* Angel put the CD into her computer and began listening to the conversation that was recorded on the CD. The first voice she recognized was Elbee's.

"Hello. Who is this?" she heard Elbee ask as the conversation began.

"This is Tasha, and I just wanted to call and say congratulations."

"Congratulations for what?"

"Your engagement."

Angel thought to herself, *Ha ha! He's my man now.*

"You play too much. What makes you think we're getting married?" Angel heard Elbee say.

"Well, either way, I wanted to say I know I hurt you, and I'm sorry. Although I miss you, I'm just glad you found love again," Tasha was saying.

"I miss you, too, sweetie. This past year without you has been hard on me."

To hear Elbee say those words made Angel's jaw drop. The tears began to roll down her face. She could not believe what she was hearing. *If Elbee didn't want to be with me, he shouldn't have proposed,* she thought as the CD continued playing.

"You don't know how many times I picked up the phone to call and ask you could I come back home. I was just scared you would tell me no."

"Baby, I wouldn't have told you no," Tasha replied.

"I wanna come home, baby" were the last words Angel heard Elbee say before the CD ended. Sitting at her desk, all Angel could do was cry.

How could Elbee do this to me? If he wants to be with that heifer, he can have her. She wiped the tears from her eyes because she was too strong now to let another man break her down.

"What up, Angel?" Blak asked, sticking his head into her office.

Angel left her seat, walked towards Blak, and burst into tears.

Here I Come, World Here I Come

Rocky was tired and excited all at the same time. As hard as he tried, he could not sleep the night before because he knew he was on that freedom train. He had spent almost two years in prison on a twenty-five year sentence, but thanks to his father and his connections, he was going home.

"Espananza, grab your shit and let's go!" the guard yelled.

Looking at his cell mate, Rocky laughed and said, "I'll holla at you on the outside, homie."

Rocky walked up to the guard's desk so he could begin being processed out of the place he had called home for as many months. He had been looking forward to this day. Now was the time for him to get his life together and settle back down with his wife.

"Espananza, I got some bad news for you," the officer said, laughing. "We seem to have misplaced your clothes."

"You know what, slim? You can keep them damn clothes. I don't want anything to remind me of the day that I ended up in this hell hole. Just lead my black ass to the door. You dig?"

As he walked towards the gates of freedom, Rocky began feeling more and more relieved. He began to breathe easier. The air began to feel lighter and smell fresher. The stench of sweat and musk started to become a lot less prevalent.

When they approached the gate for the prison, the guard looked at Rocky. "I'll see you back here within the year."

"Ha ha! Don't hold your breath waiting for that to happen, you minimum-wage-making muthafucka." Looking freedom in the face, Rocky yelled out, "Here I come, world! Here I come!"

"What up, Rock?" Tony bellowed once he saw Rocky take his first step out of prison.

"Boy, you know you my main apple scrapple. You gonna be my nigga even if you don't ever get no bigga," Rocky told Tony, giving him a hug and pound. "I hope you got some clothes for a brotha. It seems as if the employees of the good state of Georgia misplaced my nine-hundred-dollar Armani suit, but who cares. They can keep that bastard as long as I'm free."

"Fool, you know I got some fresh gear for you."

"Cool beans."

Rocky began stripping out of the orange jumpsuit that he had become accustomed to wearing. He stood outside of the prison in his underwear and t-shirt, enjoying the breeze of the May air. Tony handed Rocky some LRG jeans, a Coogi shirt, and some butter Timberland boots to put on.

"Come on, dawg. Let's get into the Suburban and get you dressed. We got a long night ahead of us," Tony told Rocky. "Oh and I got a coming home present for you."

Speak Now Or...Hold Your Piece

When Tony opened the back door to the black SUV, a beautiful, five-foot five-inch, mocha complexion young lady dressed in Victoria Secret lingerie and pumps stepped out of the truck. All that could be heard from the prisoners in the yard was, "Damn!" After showing off her perfect figure, the young lady got back into the vehicle and signaled for Rocky to follow her.

Rocky did as he was told, but not before looking the guard right in the eyes and, with a huge smile, saying, "Damn, damn, damn!"

All In

It had been several days since Angel had received the CD with Elbee's voice on it asking Tasha could he come back to her. She was ninety-nine point nine percent sure it was Tasha who had sent her the CD. Blak had assured her there was something fishy about the conversation she heard on the CD. He asked her if she could give him some time to get to the bottom of it. Against her feelings, she agreed.

As much as she wanted to confront Elbee about the CD, Blak made her promise that she wouldn't. After the way he kept her secret and helped her solve the problem, she felt she owed him a chance to find out if what she heard was true. Even though it was eating her up on the inside, she was going to hold it all together. *But Blak had better not take too long,* she thought to herself.

The ringing of the doorbell startled her and stopped the debate she had going on inside her head. She wasn't expecting anyone, and Elbee had a key. She was apprehensive about

Speak Now Or...Hold Your Piece

opening the door after looking through the peephole. All she could see were flowers and a man's hand. That made her nervous.

"Who is it?" she asked.

Elbee pulled the flowers away from his face, and with a big grin, he responded, "It's your husband-to-be. Who did you think it was?"

"Where's your key?"

"Just open the door, woman," Elbee answered back, laughing.

Angel opened the door not knowing exactly how to feel. She was excited about the flowers and the small box Elbee had in his hand, but in the back of her mind, she kept hearing his voice on the CD.

"What did I do, or better yet, what did you do for me to deserve all of this?" Angel asked sarcastically.

"Now why somebody gotta do something for you to get a gift? Why can't it be just because I love you? Why can't a brotha be happy that his building is done and he can move when he's ready, so he decided to get his woman something?" Elbee stated with a big smile.

Angel was so excited that she screamed and began jumping for joy. She knew Elbee had been working hard to get to this day. It also meant she would get her man back for serious quality time. With Angel being so excited and jumping up and down, Elbee began to do the same, looking like a little retarded kid.

"You're so silly," Angel blurted out, while watching Elbee jump around. "Elbee, can I ask you something?" she continued in a soft but serious tone.

"Sure, baby. What's up?"

Looking away from him, she proceeded. "Are you happy about our relationship and do you still want to marry me?"

Elbee had been staring at Angel, but when he heard the question, he immediately looked away. "Angel, as you know, these last few months have been really hard on me. I had a lot of pressure at work that I had to deal with, along with the strange dreams I keep having. I have been renovating my building that someone kept vandalizing. Then, to top it all off, I got resistance from the person who I needed to support me the most."

Angel flopped down on the couch and sighed. The tears were beginning to well up in her eyes.

"Elbee, I—"

Elbee cut her off. "For the past few days, I've been thinking about you, me, and us, and after some serious thought—" He leaned down close to Angel as she began to sniffle. "Angel, I'm sorry to say this, but—" He took a deep breath and swallowed hard. "Hell yeah, I'm happy with us, and I want to marry you."

Elbee took Angel's hand and put a two-carat diamond tennis bracelet on her wrist.

"I love you."

"I hate you, boy!" Angel yelled, as she began hitting Elbee playfully. "How could you do that to me? I thought you were breaking up with me."

"Now why would I do something crazy like that?"

She thought about telling him about the CD but remembered she had given her word to Blak.

"I thought you might want to get back with Tasha," she

uttered in a voice just above a whisper.

Elbee shook his head, "You don't know me as well as I thought you did if you thought that."

"I'm sorry. I just thought that—," she said, then paused. "Well, I don't know what I thought."

"Well, do me a favor and don't think, because that's not what I pay you for," Elbee chuckled.

He sat down beside Angel and held her in his arms. "Angel, I love you and I want to be with you. Only you can make me feel any different. When it comes to this love affair we have, I am all in, one hundred percent. Ya heard me?"

"Yeah, I hear you," she whispered. Then she kissed her man passionately and hoped he never found out her secret.

One Shot

Rocky looked at Deshawn lying in the bed looking worn out. Seeing her like that let him know he still had it, as he began doing his "beat it up right" dance. Their first session went so quick he felt he had to redeem himself.

The ringing of his cell phone brought him back to reality. Rocky answered the phone.

"Is she sleep yet? 'Cause we gotta go," the caller said.

"No, but she will be in a second," Rocky replied, then ended the call.

"Who was that?" Deshawn asked, rolling over.

Before she could make another sound, Rocky put a pillow over her face and fired two shots into it.

"Rock-a-bye, baby," Rocky said, as he walked out of the hotel.

Rocky pulled his hat down over his face, being careful not to be seen. Tony was in the truck outside waiting to pull off.

"You got the cleanup taken care of, right?" Rocky asked Tony.

"And you know this, mannn. The head maid is a smoker, and she has the key to the adjoining room. So, no one will be seen going into that room until morning."

"Good, good, that'll work. What's going on with that dude that Angel has been seeing? Did you have him handled?"

"I tried, but—"

Rocky began to yell. "What do you mean tried? You were supposed to have someone whoop that nigga's ass real good!"

"As I was saying, I tried to use one of our usual people, but everyone kept saying the dude is connected. So, I used a young dude that was trying to make a name for himself."

"So what happened?"

"Rock, dude beat the shit outta that young boy. To be honest, I say we just take that nigga out with a few hot ones instead of trying to fight him."

Tony looked straight ahead as he continued driving to the airport. He was hoping Rocky listened to him, because he was not going to have a chance in hell to beat Angel's new man in a fist fight.

"So you really think we should have him rock-a-byed?"

"If that dude is connected like everyone is saying he is, I think we should go ahead and do that."

"Who is he down with?" Rocky asked.

"That's the thing. No one knows. The word on the block is that if anyone puts hands on that dude, there's going to be some consequences and repercussions."

"Alright. Well, call in the hit, and don't use any of our people. If this dude is connected, we don't want to start a war if they miss, and Pops would lose his mind if we did. So, make sure you use someone good because we will only get one shot at this guy."

Tony made the call as they were pulling into the airport parking lot. Rocky wondered who Angel had gotten involved with that had so much clout that no one wanted to touch him. Well, if he only had one shot at him, he damn sure would make it was a good one. No one was going to keep him away from Angel.

Kegels

Angel stood by the bathroom door staring at Elbee while he laid in the bed sleeping. This was the first time in months she saw him resting so peacefully. Although she did not want to wake him, she longed for some of the attention that only he could give her body.

As she began to undress before getting back into the bed with her man, the thought of the CD popped into her head. She was about to abandon the thought of being intimate with Elbee, when the light from the bathroom hit her new tennis bracelet and shined a pretty blue light into her eyes. Then she heard Blak's words: *There is something fishy about this CD.* At that moment, the feeling of love and wanting rushed her body.

Elbee was rolling onto his stomach when Angel approached the bed naked as the day she was born. She straddled him at his waist and began massaging his muscular back while gyrating slowly on him. The moistness of Angel's womanhood began to arouse Elbee. After being massaged for several minutes, he started to relax as he let out a sensual moan.

Feeling she had Elbee's complete attention, Angel leaned forward, pressing her breasts against his back, and began licking his freshly shaved bald head. Although Elbee had mentioned many times about how much he liked having his head licked, Angel had never done it before. Now that she was doing it, the response she was getting from her man was turning her on.

Elbee lay feeling like he was about to poke a hole in the mattress. He was so excited. He wanted to participate in this sexual expedition so badly, but the soft tender kisses that Angel was placing on his head had him paralyzed. Finally getting his bearings, he slowly rolled over onto his back.

"I see everyone is up," Angel remarked slyly.

"Yes, we are, and since none of us have anywhere to be today, we think you oughta put us back to sleep."

"I think I can handle that."

Angel took both her feet, placed them on the bed, and squatted over Elbee. Using both hands, she inserted his hardened soldier inside of her moist and throbbing vagina. Then she slowly moved up and down on his dick like she was riding a seesaw.

Elbee laid back and enjoyed every minute that Elbee Jr. got to explore Angel's womanhood. As she got more and more caught up in their lovemaking, she began using the muscles in her vagina to tighten up on his penis. It felt so good that it took everything Elbee had in him not to explode.

"Oh shit, oh shit. Two plus two is four. Four plus four is eight."

Slowly coming up for another stroke, Angel looked at Elbee and smiled. "What's wrong, baby?" she asked and slowly went back down.

Speak Now Or... Hold Your Piece

"Noth...noth...nothing," he stuttered, taking a deep breath. "Keep doing what chu doing."

Coming back up and squeezing again, she asked, "Are you sure? I've never heard you do addition while we were making love before." She then slid down his pole once again.

With his eyes on the verge of rolling back in his head, he replied, "You have never squeezed your sugar walls around my dick before either."

Coming back up and squeezing again, she said, "They are called Keigels. I read about them in one of the books you gave me and started practicing." She slid back down and slowly came back up. "Do you like them?"

"Why, yes. Yes, I do."

"Well, since you do, let me show you a few things."

Going down again, Angel began to quicken her pace. In rhythm, Elbee started moving with her. When Angel came down, Elbee would come up to meet her in mid stroke.

"Ooh, Elbee, that's my spot. That's my spot."

They continued making love, slowing down and picking up the pace for another ten minutes until they each climaxed.

In a sensual voice, Angel remarked, "Elbee, you make me feel so loved."

Rolling over to go to sleep, he replied, "That's my job."

Your Worst Nightmare

Elbee was as tired as a one-legged man in an ass kicking contest. Not only had it been a long, trying day, but he was drained from the sexcapades of the night before. Riding with the windows down and letting the spring breeze hit him in the face was the only he felt he was going to make it home. It was times like these that he was glad he didn't have allergies.

As he turned onto the street of his new home, he reached out and turned his music down. The excitement of having his own home again was starting to finally set in. Living with Blak was cool, but he could hear the words of his favorite uncle in his ears: *There is nothing like having your own.* Elbee looked up to the sky, kissed his two fingers, and raised them up to Tru Marshall Sr., the man he gave the credit to making him the man that he was.

After pulling into the parking space he had designated for himself, Elbee just sat in his automobile looking at his new home. He turned the ignition to shut the engine of his SUV off,

Speak Now Or...Hold Your Piece

and when he stepped out of his truck, he found someone waiting for him.

"I got your ass now, muthafucka," the voice snarled, putting a gun to Elbee's head.

"Go 'head with all that playing, Blak? I'm tired and trying to go to bed," Elbee responded.

"I ain't Blak, nigga. I'm your worst nightmare," the man hissed, spinning Elbee around and putting his loaded 9mm pistol in his face.

After looking at the man's face, any fear of getting shot left his mind. He realized it was the young dude from the club.

Elbee started laughing. "Nigga, please. If you gonna shoot me, then do it before I get upset and beat your ass again."

Getting upset that Elbee had laughed at him, he smacked Elbee across the face with his gun. Elbee stumbled back against his truck and spit the blood out of his mouth. *This young teenage mutant ninja turtle has gone too far,* Elbee thought. If he was going to die tonight, he was going to die like a man. He was going to die fighting.

Leaning against the truck a little longer than he needed to, Elbee started to formulate a plan. He had watched enough *Law and Order* and *CSI* to know he needed to get some of this guy's DNA on him somehow.

Elbee stood straight up and spit some of the blood that was gushing into his mouth into his assailant's face. When the blood hit the stranger's face, he flinched and turned his head. Seeing that the man had flinched, Elbee threw a punch that connected squarely on his attacker's chin. Feeling all of the two hundred pounds that Elbee had put behind the punch, the guy dropped his gun and fell to the ground.

"Oh shit, let me find out your punk ass can't take a punch!" Elbee barked, as he started kicking the stranger.

Elbee had kicked the stranger three times, when he felt something cold against his neck. During the ruckus, Elbee hadn't noticed the stranger had a partner.

"Don't kick him again," the voice cautioned. "Get up, nigga. You can't even kill somebody that you got the drop on. You're a waste of a good nut."

The coldness of the second man could be heard in his voice. Elbee knew if he tried anything with this guy, someone was definitely going to die.

"Look, man, if it's money you want, I don't have any on me," Elbee spoke calmly.

"Nigga, don't nobody want your money. We want your blood."

The hammer on the stranger's gun was cocked, and he was ready to pull the trigger.

"Now, son, I advise you not to pull that trigger. If you do, I promise you when you go to prison, you will have a much bigger asshole than the one you got now, because that's where I'm going to shoot you, ya little Yankee muthafucka."

When he turned around, Elbee saw Ricky standing there with his gun ready to shoot someone. At that moment, he took the liberty to punch the second stranger in the mouth, and he continued punching him until he fell. After kicking him several times, Elbee took the gun and stuck it in the stranger's mouth.

"Nigga, do you know me? Do you know who the hell you're dealing with? I will blow your fuckin' brains out all over that nigga's shoes and then blow his little tallywhacker off."

Ricky watched as Elbee looked like he was getting ready to

pull the trigger. "Don't do it, Elbee. These punks aren't worth it."

When the police showed up and arrested the two strangers, Elbee thought, *This was supposed to be an easy night. None of this was supposed to happen.*

Elbee then looked at Ricky and said, "I need a drink."

Can't Win for Losing

Giving Elbee a pound and laughing, Blak inquired, "How was the first night in the new place, and when you coming to get your junk?"

"Man, you're not even gonna believe what happened to me last night," Elbee responded.

"What happened? Did you call those two lesbian hotties that I met over for a threesome in the new house?"

Elbee sat for a second remembering the day he had met the two lesbians who liked to have threesomes with men. When he met them, they were on the hunt for a man who they both could be with and who would understand they only wanted him for sex. The idea of a threesome excited Elbee, so he agreed. However, that one night of passion turned into a couple years of spontaneous sexcapades.

"Boy, why you and DB always think I'm doing some freak stuff?"

"Because you are," Blak replied, laughing.

Speak Now Or...Hold Your Piece

"Well, that's not it this time."

"So what happened, dawg?" Blak pushed.

"Some bamas tried to take me out last night."

"Take you out! You mean them niggas were trying to kill you?"

"Hell yeah, and if it wasn't for Ricky, there would have been some slow singing and flower bringing today."

"What the hell is going on? Do you know them bamas and that's why they're beefing with you?"

Elbee thought for a second. "I had beef with one of them fools at the club about a month back. Now that I think about it, the other dude was with the guy that rolled up on us that day we were in front of my building. Blak, something is up, and I need to find out what it is."

"Well, while you're doing that, you might want to check into this CD," Blak continued, handing Elbee the CD. "It has a conversation on it with you telling Tasha that you want to come back to her."

"What!" Elbee exclaimed, frowning up his face.

"Yeah, you heard me. The CD has Elbee's greatest phrases on it."

"Where did you get it from?" he asked.

"I got it from Angel, who got it from a so-called anonymous source."

Hearing that, it started to become clear to Elbee why Angel asked him the questions she did. His blood began to boil and anger started to consume his body. Why couldn't this heifer just leave him alone?

"Man, that broad just won't quit. So what did Angel say when she heard this fraggle naggle bull?" Elbee asked, while pacing in his office.

"She cried and threatened to call off the wedding."

Plopping down in his chair, Elbee said, "I swear if it ain't one thing it's another. First, somebody trashes my spot. Next, Saundra dropped a bomb on me. Then, I got niggas tryin' to kill me. Now, I gotta deal with this bullshit! It seems like every time I take two steps forward I get knocked three steps back. I can't win for losing, but that's okay because I will deal with Tasha's stankin' ass."

"Well, handle your business, pimpin'. Just handle your business," Blak reiterated as he left Elbee's office.

Reaching for his phone, Elbee replied, "Oh, I am. Believe me, I am."

I Got You

"Okay."

"What are they saying?"

"Cool. I'll handle things from here," Tony said, ending his call.

"Did they take that nigga out?" Rocky asked.

"Not exactly," Tony answered.

"What do you mean not exactly?" Rocky snapped.

"They got locked up trying to take him out."

Rocky lost it when he heard they had missed their shot.

"How fuckin' hard is it to put the squeeze on one muthafucka? Who is this nigga that none of our regular hitters ain't tryin' to make no bread to take his ass out? I guess I gotta handle this dude myself!" Rocky ranted.

"Rock, you can't do that, dawg," Tony pleaded.

"And why not?" Rocky yelled. "When did we start letting some punk-ass nigga we don't know dictate how we do business?"

"Rock, I told you the word on the street is that this fool is connected and untouchable. Now, your pops has been meeting with some people here in DC, and I don't know what it's about. But, if we do something to mess up any business deals he may be working on all over some bitch, he's gonna deal with us both," Tony protested.

In a fit of rage, Rocky pulled his gun out and pointed it in Tony's face. "Nigga, don't you ever in your life call my wife a bitch again! You hear me?"

"So what you gonna do, kill me nigga? Well, if that's the case, do it then!" Tony snarled, as he walked towards Rocky and pressed his head against the barrel of the gun. "I'm a fuckin' soldier, fool, so yo gun don't scare me, nigga," he continued while pounding on his chest. "If you gonna do it, go 'head and pull the trigga."

Realizing the mistake he was making, Rocky began to calm down. To pull a gun on his best friend for being right was stupid. Calling Angel a bitch was out of line, but knowing Tony the way he did, he knew he did that only to get his point across. If they jumped out of the window and did something to mess up his pop's money, he was not going to be happy, and there would be a lot of questions to answer.

Rocky lowered his gun. "My bad, dawg. I was wrong for that, but you ain't gotta be calling my girl a bitch."

"That's cool, but, dude, I need you to stay focused through all of this shit. To your pops, you're family. I'm just another worker who he will kill faster than you can blink. So, we gotta be smart on how we deal with this fool."

"Okay, but I wanna see this dude who I can't kill for sleeping with my wife. Where can I find him?"

Speak Now Or...Hold Your Piece

"Rock, I know where we can find him, but you gotta stay cool, dawg. We can't afford to start anything."

"I got you. I got you."

"No, I mean it. Whoever is protecting this dude is well connected."

"I know, I know. I got you, Tony. No trouble."

"Oh and, Rock, if you ever pull a gun on me again, you better use it. Because if you don't, I promise you that I'm gonna use mine!"

Pressure Burst Pipes

The time had come for Elbee to face the music. The paternity test had confirmed what Saundra had told him. There was a ninety-nine point nine percent chance he was her baby's daddy. He had been dealing with that truth for weeks, and now it was time for him to sit down and talk with Saundra.

Saundra was in Elbee's driveway, sitting in her car and contemplating leaving. She was ashamed but knew one day she would have to face Elbee and tell him about JR, and now was the time.

Elbee was finishing up some painting and Remy, when he heard a knock on the door. He knew it was Saundra, and boy, did he have a lot of questions for her. He just hoped the few shots of Remy he had would help keep him calm.

"Hey, Saundra, come on in. Excuse the mess. I'm still putting the finishing touches on the place before I move in," Elbee told her.

"So this is your place?"

Speak Now Or...Hold Your Piece

"Yep. I bought the building and had Benny remodel it."

"Wow, that's great. I always knew you would do some big things."

"Oh, so is that why you kept my son from me for fifteen fucking years?" Elbee declared with anger in his voice.

"I see you haven't changed much. You still get straight to the point."

"Saundra, I have a son that's fifteen years old who I just found out about. So what do you want me to do? Just sit around and shoot the shit with you like nothing has happened? If that's what you thought, I'm not. I want to know why you didn't tell me."

Just then, Elbee heard a noise like somebody was at his door. After everything that had been going on in the neighborhood, he grabbed his gun and went to the door. He opened the door and looked around, but he didn't see anyone.

"Look, Elbee, I know you're mad, but you have to let me explain," Saundra continued.

"Dogs get mad. Me? I'm angry as hell. I have a son that probably thinks I'm a piece of shit deadbeat dad because he has never seen or heard from me before."

"Elbee, I understand you're angry, but believe me when I say that I have never let JR think badly about you. There has been a birthday and a Christmas present from you every year. I made sure of that. I just need you to let me explain why I did what I did."

Elbee sat down on a bucket of paint and put his hands behind his ears. "I'm listening."

Saundra smiled at him. "You were always able to make me smile. That's why I always loved you."

"Saundra, your lips are moving and noise is coming out, but you ain't saying nothing."

"As you already know, the night before you left for basic training we made love. What you don't know is that was the first time I had been with anyone sexually."

"I was your first? I thought that punk Alex was your first. He was telling everyone that he had sex with you."

"He didn't even get to smell it let alone hit it. You were my first, and a couple of weeks after you left, I found out I was pregnant."

"Why didn't you tell me? Saundra, that night we spent together meant the world to me."

"I didn't tell you because I didn't want you to think I was trying to trap you."

"I would have never thought that about you. You were the first woman that I ever truly loved."

"If that was the case, then why didn't you ever call me, Elbee?" Saundra asked, starting to cry.

"Because when I first got to basic training, I wasn't allowed to use the phone. So, I wrote you every day, but you never wrote me back. I just figured you had met someone and didn't want to be bothered with me."

"Elbee, I didn't write back because I knew I would have told you about the baby. From your letters, I could tell you already had enough pressure on you without me."

Elbee walked over to Saundra, wiped the tears from her eyes, and held her in his arms. "Pressure burst pipes, and I promise you that I ain't no pipe. Plus, you could never pressure me. So when do I get to meet my son?"

Ladies' Night

It was the last Friday of the month, and Angel, Carolyn, and Rhonda were getting together for their ladies' night of pampering. They had scheduled for someone to come and do manicures, pedicures, and facials. Like always, Carolyn and Angel were waiting for Rhonda.

"Did you talk to Rhonda today, Angel?"

"Yeah and she told me that she would be here on time, but you see she is late as usual."

"Rhonda is definitely one of those people that Granddaddy was talking about. That girl is gonna be late for her own funeral."

The doorbell ringing broke up their laughter.

"I bet these are the people to do the spa treatment," Angel stated.

"Where did you find these people? You know the last ones you got were just awful."

As she was walking to the door, Angel responded, "Elbee set this all up. These are some people that he knows about."

"What does Elbee know about manicures and pedicures?" Carolyn asked sarcastically.

"Girl, that man gets his hands done every two weeks and a pedicure plus a facial once a month. I told him once we get married he has to put me on his schedule for the same thing."

"So how much is it? I need to make sure I have enough cash."

"Don't worry. Elbee has already paid for it and gave them a nice tip."

When Angel opened the door, standing in front of her were three of the finest men that she had ever seen. They all stood about 6'1" to 6'3" tall. Two of them had a milk chocolate complexion. One was bald and the other had a nice close cut. The third one was black as the midnight sky with some of the best looking dreads she had ever seen on a man.

"May I help you?" Angel asked.

The man with the dreads answered in a baritone voice, "Yes, we're here to see Ms. Angel Terry."

"I'm Ms. Terry. How can I help you?"

"My man Elbee hired us to provide pampering for you and your friends this evening."

Rhonda walked up just as the man was finishing his sentence. "Well, it's ladies' night, and I got champagne and orange juice. So you brothas can go ahead and get to pampering," she chimed, as she walked into the house. "Sorry I'm late, ladies, but y'all know how I am."

Angel and Carolyn gave Rhonda a hug as they prepared for their pampering. After the guys brought in their equipment and had the ladies all set up for their pedicures, they removed their shirts. The ladies looked at the men and began to swoon. They could not believe how muscular these men were.

"Girl, these men must have been sculptured by God himself," Rhonda commented, while giving Carolyn five.

"My man is fine, but damn, you brothas are foine, as Blak would say," Carolyn added.

"Elbee would have a fit if he knew some half-naked man was touching my feet," Angel chimed in.

"I don't think he would be too upset," one of the guys replied, while making his pectoral muscles move, "because he paid us to do your spa treatment this way."

"I knew I loved that boy for a reason," Rhonda sighed as the bald brother rubbed her feet.

The ladies laughed and talked while drinking mimosas all evening. They enjoyed the pampering they received, but more importantly, they enjoyed the bond of sisterhood that had been formed between them.

After filling their glasses with some mimosa, Angel held her glass up to make a toast.

"Here's to the two best friends and bridesmaids a person could have. I love you both."

"Awww," Rhonda and Carolyn sang together, 'and we love you, too."

"I'm just glad you were there to help Elbee get over Tasha after that fiasco of a relationship. Oh and for the record, I never liked that girl."

"After the CD I heard, I'm not sure Elbee feels the same way," Angel mumbled.

"Yeah, DB told me about that CD. Girl, I promise you that you don't have anything to worry about. I have known Elbee since high school, and believe me when I say that once that brotha moves on, he has moved on."

"I believe you, Rhonda, but something has been different about him lately."

"Trust and believe me when I say if Elbee wanted out of your relationship, you would be the first to know. Now, that's enough of this nonsense. We have a wedding to plan."

"Amen to that," Carolyn echoed.

Rhonda had reassured Angel about Elbee's love for her. Rhonda just hoped Angel's love for him was going to be strong enough to withstand hearing that he had a fifteen-year-old son.

More Than Meets the Eye

Rocky walked into the gym ready to see the man that he felt had ruined his marriage, the dude that he couldn't seem to be able to get rid of without a conflict.

"Excuse me, sir, but it cost seven dollars to get in for the day, or you need to fill out paperwork to get an extended membership," the young lady at the counter said with an attitude.

Rocky was taken aback by the way the young lady had approached him. Apparently, she didn't know who he was and what type of pull he had. Since she didn't, he was going to let her know.

Tony saw Rocky getting ready to go off on the young lady and stepped in. "It's okay, Ms. Lady. I got him. We just need passes for today."

Rocky looked at Tony strangely as they walked into the gym. "What the hell is wrong with that hoodrat? She must not know who I am."

"Rock, you're in DC. You ain't got no fuckin' pull or clout

here, nigga. So, no, she doesn't know yo black ass."

Rocky and Tony walked around the gym for a few minutes and even tried to use a couple of the machines before they found a spot back off to the side. That's when Tony noticed Elbee walking into the gym.

"That's him right there, Rock," Tony said, pointing at Elbee.

Rocky looked on as Elbee walked past the girl at the counter, and she just smiled at him like he owned the place. He noticed when he and Tony had asked the guy about getting a couple of towels they were told there weren't any available. Yet, he freely gave Elbee two fresh towels when he walked by and he didn't even have to ask for them. Rocky sat trying to figure out what it was about Elbee that he was missing, because everyone in the gym spoke to him and treated him like he was some type of celebrity.

"Tony, who is this nigga? Everyone in here is treating him like he's Will Smith or somebody. He gotta be moving some major weight."

"If he is, nobody knows about it. Word on the street is he's just an ordinary Joe Shmoe. I did hear that he's supposed to be some neighborhood basketball legend that never made it big."

Elbee walked over to use the same elliptical machine that Rocky had tried to use only minutes ago but was told he couldn't. As Rocky watched Elbee working out, he couldn't believe he was being treated like a chump for a nobody.

"Tony, there's more to this bastard than meets the eye. They treat this fool the way they treat me at home. Get on the phone and have this nigga thoroughly checked out."

"Aw'ight, Rock, will do. You ready to leave?"

"Nope, I wanna check this nigga out some more." As Rocky

Speak Now Or...Hold Your Piece

kept staring at Elbee, he mumbled, "Yep, I'm gonna have to kill this muthafucka myself."

Splaining to Do

Elbee had just finished riding the bike when Saundra walked into the gym. Today was the day Elbee was finally going to meet his son. He had never feared anything in his life before, but he was terrified about meeting his son and how he would react to him.

He took a big swallow of water and got off the bike. As he walked towards Saundra, he noticed his cousin Benny and the rest of his boys were entering the building. Today was the day he was going to let all of his boys know he had a son.

"What's going on, Ms. Lady?" Elbee stated, giving Saundra a hug.

"Nothing much," she replied, holding onto Elbee a little longer than she should have while inhaling his scent. "Are you ready to meet your son, because you look nervous?"

"I am nervous. Hell, I'm meeting my fifteen-year-old son for the first time. But, I ain't never run from responsibility, and I ain't about to pick today to start running."

Kissing him lightly on his cheek, she whispered, "I know.

That's why I still love you."

"What the hell! Is this little Saundra?" Benny asked, walking up.

"Yes, it is. I see the gang is all here," she said, giving all the guys a hug.

"Hey, Ma. I'm here with some of the fellas. So what's up? Why did you want me to meet you here?"

Elbee looked at the five-foot eight-inch tall, caramel complexioned, handsome young man that stood before him. Even if he hadn't taken a paternity test, there would have been no way he could deny that this young man was his son. Looking at him, he saw a spitting image of himself when he was that age. The look on his friends' faces let him know he wasn't going to have to tell them anything. They already knew.

"Who is it that you wanted me to meet?" JR asked.

"Well, baby, you're always talking about Benjamin Nessprin. You didn't believe I knew him, so I thought you might like to meet him."

Excited about the possibility of meeting a neighborhood legend, JR replied, "Ma, you know I would!"

"Well, how about you and your boys running against him and his squad," Benny interjected.

"That would be cool," JR responded.

Extending his hand out to him, Benny said, "I'm Benjamin Nessprin. So, let's ball."

This was the chance of a lifetime. Everyone in the neighborhood talked about how good Benny was and could have been before he got locked up, and how it was a shame his little cousin quit playing after Benny got convicted. Georgetown would have been a lock for the finals with both of them. JR felt if he and his friends could beat them, they would make a real name for themselves.

"Now all we need is for your cousin to show up so I can bust his tail. Then Coach Brown can stop saying how good he was and that I should play more like him," JR said to his boys.

"Well, lil homie, one part of your wish is going to come true. I don't know about you busting my tail, though," Elbee told him, while walking towards the court.

Benny pulled Elbee to the side as they were getting ready to play the game. "Cuz, is there something you wanna tell a brotha?" he whispered.

"I will tell you everything after we whip my son and his friends' asses in this game."

"We gonna do that, but then, boooy, you got some splaining to do."

Ballin'

"Check ball," Elbee said, tossing JR the ball.

"Are you sure you wanna give us the ball first? This might be the last time you old timers get to touch the ball," JR chided, laughing with his buddies.

Benny, DB, Blak, and Ramon all looked at Elbee and shook their heads. The more JR talked, the more everyone knew he was Elbee's son. All Elbee could think was that playing JR and his friends was Saundra's idea.

JR passed the ball to one of his friends, and they began to move the ball up the floor. After making a few passes around the court, they gave the ball back to JR, who shot a fifteen-foot jumper over Elbee.

Two more trips up and down the floor, and JR had stolen the ball once and then scored over Elbee again on the next one. Benny and DB were looking at Elbee while shaking their heads. They could see he wasn't playing his game. He was playing soft.

When JR came down and scored over Elbee one more time,

he looked at his mother and yelled, "Ballinnnn'," while holding his hand up like rapper Jim Jones. "I hope this ain't the dude that coach thinks I should play, because he suuuuucks."

It was at that moment that the complexity of the game changed. Things got real.

"Oh, that's ballin'? Okay then, you young thunder cat. Get your pen and paper ready because I'm about to show you ballin'," Elbee barked.

Elbee licked his fingers and smacked the ball. "Ball game, fellas."

"Well, it's about damn time!" Benny snapped. "Six to one, them."

Elbee dribbled the ball up the court using his strength to keep JR off balance. He knew there was no way JR could outmuscle him. Every time JR tried to get close to him, Elbee would use his forearm to push him back.

Benny was getting ready to set a pick for Elbee, but he waved him off. He was intent on scoring on JR without any help. Elbee got JR down in the post, made a quick drop step move to the left, spun to the right, and layed the ball up off the glass.

"And one!" Elbee yelled. "Ding! Ding! School is in session," Elbee chuckled, tossing JR the ball.

"That's just one point, pops," JR said, bringing the ball up the court.

"Boy, don't you know you're trying to play pity pat with a chess player," Elbee shot back.

"That's my dawg. That's my dawg," Blak interjected.

JR tried to shake Elbee with a crossover dribble. That's when Elbee stole the ball and raced up the court with JR and

Speak Now Or...Hold Your Piece

Benny trailing him. JR thought he was going to block Elbee's shot, but Elbee tossed the ball off the backboard to Benny for a dunk, causing to the gym to erupt.

"I hope that wasn't your attempt at a crossover, because it suuuuucked," Elbee laughed.

Elbee definitely had his head in the game. He tossed DB an alley-oop on a fast break. He hit Blak with a bounce pass for a layup and then he swung a cross court pass to Ramon for a fifteen-foot jumper.

The game had changed dramatically. No matter what JR and his friends tried, they couldn't stop the onslaught that Elbee and the guys were putting on them.

"Fifteen to nine. Point game, fellas!" DB boasted, calling out the score.

JR looked at Elbee. "You got a little handle, pops. You can even play some defense, but you can't score."

Elbee checked the ball half court. "I might not be able to score, but you can't guard me, young buck."

Elbee passed the ball to Benny. Knowing that Elbee had something to prove, Benny passed the ball back to him. All the guys realized what was going on, so they cleared the lane so Elbee and JR could go one on one.

Elbee began dribbling the ball, trying to figure out how he was going to score the last point. He dribbled hard to the basket and JR stuck with him. So, Elbee backed the ball out and went hard to the basket again. Before JR could make a move to steal the ball, Elbee crossed over to the left quickly, pulled up, and shot a quick jumper that was nothing but net.

With his hand held up in the air, Elbee said, "Now that's ballin'."

Elbee meet Elbee

"Good game, youngster. You're pretty good, and with a little more work, one day you might be as good as me," Elbee told JR, giving him a pound.

Saundra came down out of the bleachers to where Elbee and her son were standing. Seeing her son and his father together for the first time was a beautiful sight to her. She had waited so long for this day to come, and it was finally here.

Everyone was starting to get together for another game. Elbee looked at Saundra as he was walking back on the floor, and he could tell this was the moment he would officially meet his son.

"Yo, El, let's ball!" DB yelled.

"Pick someone else up. I got to take care of something," Elbee replied.

"JR, we need to speak with you for a moment," Saundra said to him nervously.

"Okay, Ma, what's up?"

"Elbee Elton Thompson, I would like for you to meet Elbee

Speak Now Or...Hold Your Piece

Elton Nessprin, your father," Saundra blurted out, then dropped her head.

JR stood quiet for a moment as he took in what his mother had just said to him. There were so many questions that immediately began swirling around in his head that his knees got weak.

JR looked at Elbee. "So where the fuck you been for the last fifteen years of my life? What happened? You started hearing my name around town and the fact that they're getting ready to rank me as the number one point guard in the country, so you decide to show up?"

"JR!" Saundra snapped. "Watch your mouth and your tone, young man. I did not raise you to speak to adults in such a manner."

"That's right, Ma. *You*," he said, putting emphasis on the word 'you', "didn't raise me to speak to adults that way. Now where have you been?"

"It's cool, Saundra. He deserves some answers, and I'm willing to give them to him," Elbee interjected, noticing that people were starting to stare. "But, instead of here can we go somewhere to sit down and talk?"

"Why wait? Do you need time to make up a few lies about why you haven't been around?"

The question cut like a knife. Although he had just found out about his son, Elbee still felt the sting of his words and the bitterness of his anger. This was a conversation Elbee had promised himself that he would never have with his children. Now, here he was doing just that.

"JR, he doesn't have to lie about where he has been. Baby, your father—"

Elbee interrupted Saundra. "I'm not gonna lie to you, son, but now is not the time to really hold this discussion."

"Well, when is the time, Dad? You haven't done anything but send me some gifts. They were nice gifts, but they were just gifts for fifteen years."

"I guess now will have to be the time then. When I was young and dumb, your mother and I spent a wonderful night together," Elbee said, looking at Saundra as she began to blush. "At the time, I had no idea what being a man meant, and I knew she deserved better than what I could offer her. So, I disappeared."

"But I received gifts from you for everything, so you knew where I was," JR challenged.

"Your mother bought those gifts and put my name on them so you wouldn't think badly about me. So, when I bumped into your mother, she told me about you. Now I'm here, and although I may never be the father that you wanted, I would at least like to be your friend."

"Is all of this true, Ma?"

Saundra looked at her son with love in her eyes. "Yes, baby. That's what happened. Son, your father is a good man, and if he had known about you before now, there wouldn't have been anything to keep him away from you. So, for me, give him a chance." While giving her son a hug, Saundra looked at Elbee and mouthed thank you.

JR looked Elbee up and down, and then with a smile, he said, "My pops is Elbee Nessprin. So that would make Benny Nessprin my folks, too, huh? No wonder I ball so nice." He then paused before saying, "Now, Pops, don't think because I'm smiling things are cool. I got a lot of questions."

Speak Now Or...Hold Your Piece

"That's cool. For now, though, let me introduce you to my folks," Elbee replied, laughing as he thought about how JR was really like him.

Nice Night

Elbee walked into the Fish Market Restaurant in Clinton, Maryland, and saw Tasha sitting right where he knew she would be sitting. As always, she was all smiles in some man's face. That was something that had annoyed Elbee while they were together. In her eyes, it was alright for a guy to be all smiles and laughs with her, but if she even thought another woman was smiling at him, he needed to be prepared for the prelude to World War IV when they got home.

While standing there looking at Tasha, Elbee thought back to a party he and Tasha had attended when they were together. The party was at her cousin's house, and she didn't think Elbee would know anyone there.

When they got to the party, Tasha introduced Elbee to some people. Then she pointed at some other people and told him something about them. One of the girls that Tasha pointed out to Elbee looked familiar to him. When Tasha told him that her name was Dee, Elbee remembered he knew her from school and

Speak Now Or...Hold Your Piece

used to like her, but they never got together. After Elbee shared that information with Tasha, she proceeded to tell him that she was gay. Once Elbee heard that, he understood why they never hooked up.

Elbee got a chance to speak to Dee later on during the evening while Tasha was laughing it up with a few of her male friends. To Elbee, they were two old classmates just catching up on things, so he felt everything was cool. Especially since they both liked women. On the way home from the party, all hell broke loose, though.

"You knew a lot of women at the party!" Tasha snapped.

"Okay and you knew a lot of men. So what's the big deal?"

"The big deal is that I didn't spend most of the night talking to another woman," Tasha shot back.

"What other woman? I know you're not talking about Dee."

"Well, you said you tried to get with her when you were in school."

"Yeah, I did say that, but I didn't because she likes pussy as much as I do. So, that's not gonna work. Ya think?"

"Then why were you two talking all night?"

"I don't know. Maybe because we're friends!"

Tasha went on about the incident for two more hours after that. Thinking back to that incident, Elbee felt he should have gotten out of that relationship then. He didn't, and now he needed to confront the crazy broad. Although Elbee didn't like to make public scenes, it was the only way Tasha was going to understand what he was saying.

Elbee walked over and tapped Tasha on the shoulder. "That was some fucked up shit you tried to pull."

"I don't know what you're talking 'bout, boo," Tasha

responded, trying to sound innocent.

"Whatever, Tasha. Don't play with me. I know you sent Angel the CD, but that's cool, though, because it brought us closer together. As a matter of fact, we had some of the best sex ever after we listened to your lil' CD."

As Elbee finished talking to Tasha, Linda and Veronica, two of his close friends, walked over.

Elbee continued, "But just know the next time you pull a stunt like that, I'm gonna let Linda and Veronica tap that ass. Now try me."

"Whatever!" Tasha yelled.

"It's not whatever," Veronica shot back. "I promise if you keep fucking with my boy, I'm gonna beat that ass." Then Veronica took her finger and pushed Tasha in the forehead. "You have a nice night, ya hear."

.

What Do You Have in Mind

Rocky slid through the door of the Fish Market Restaurant and grabbed a seat at the bar. He had been following Elbee since he left the gym, trying to see what type of information he could find out about him. After following him for five hours, he still couldn't understand why people treated Elbee so good. The only thing he knew was that he wasn't in the game, because anyone in the game would have noticed someone was following them all day.

Rocky could see that Elbee was cordial and extremely engaging, but to him, that couldn't be the reason everyone liked Elbee so much. Rocky remembered his pops saying to him, "Son, it's better to be respected than to be feared." It wasn't until this very day that he began to realize what he was talking about. After the abuse he had taken from his biological father, Rocky had vowed that people may not respect him, but they would definitely fear him.

As Rocky sat watching the exchange between Elbee and Tasha, he was intrigued. Elbee hadn't lost his cool with anyone all day until he spoke to her. There was something between the two of them. Only a woman that you are sleeping with or had slept with can have that type of effect on a man. He had to find out what was going on between Tasha and Elbee to see if he could exploit it.

Once Elbee had left the restaurant, Rocky slid next to Tasha.

"Do you want me to catch him and beat his ass?" Rocky asked, flashing his pearly white smile.

"No, thank you," Tasha replied, while turning to look Rocky in his green eyes.

"Are you sure? Because a woman as fine as you should be adored and not threatened," Rocky continued, still smiling.

Tasha was mesmerized by Rocky's soft green eyes and enticing smile.

Extending his hand, he said, "Hello, my name is Rocky Espananza."

"I'm Tasha," she told him, responding with a smile. "Thank you for the compliment, but can I ask how did a brotha so chocolate get a Hispanic name?"

Still smiling, he replied, "Damn, you just jump right into a brotha's bizness, don't you? But, if you must know, I was adopted and my father is Hispanic. Now it's my turn."

"Okay, go ahead."

"Who was that brotha giving you such a hard time?" Rocky queried, fishing for information.

"He's my fiancé."

Rocky raised his eyebrows while giving Tasha a disturbed look.

"Well, he was my fiancé," Tasha uttered.

"After the way he acted towards you, I would hope he was

Speak Now Or... Hold Your Piece

your ex and not your current."

"He's just upset right now because I let the woman he's supposedly engaged to know we're getting back together."

Hearing those words, Rocky knew he had finally met the right person in this town. Now all he had to do was figure out a way to approach her for help.

"I can understand that, because my ex-wife is getting ready to marry some other guy even though she's still in love with me."

"Why did you two get divorced, if I may ask?"

"If you couldn't, it would be too late because you already asked," Rocky answered as they both laughed. "I had a few problems with the law and was supposed to be locked-up for twenty-five years. I just beat the charges on appeal, and now I want my wife back."

"So where are you from?" Tasha asked. "You have a strong southern drawl."

"I'm from Georgia, and I came to DC looking for my wife, Angel Terry. Her best friend told me that she moved to this area," Rocky replied, thinking he had found his opening.

Tasha looked at Rocky and smiled. "You must think I'm Boo-Boo the Fool. I love your pretty green eyes and all, but there's no way you're gonna make me believe that us meeting is a coincidence. So what's the deal, homie?"

Rocky liked Tasha's directness. "Well, since you wanna get straight to the point, here's the truth. I want my wife back and you want Elbee back, so why don't we work together so we can both get what we want?"

"So what do you have in mind?"

Grandbaby

"Hey, Ma," Elbee said, walking into his mother's house with JR in tow.

"Hey, baby, I didn't expect to see you today. I talked to Angel, and she told me that you were supposed to be getting fitted for your tux. So what are you up to, sneaky?" Elbee's mother asked, as she gave him a hug.

"I ain't up to nothing," he replied, sounding like he would when he was a child. "I came by because I wanted to introduce you to somebody."

"Boy, I hope it ain't some skank, because you know you supposed to be getting married in a couple days. Let me get my glasses."

Barbara Louise Nessprin was a matriarch in the family. There was her and Elbee's favorite aunt, Dee-Dee. His aunt Dee-Dee was the enforcer, and his mother was the voice of reason. Either way, when one of them spoke, the whole family listened. What Barbara was best known for was being Elbee's number one girl. There was no denying he was a momma's boy.

Barbara put her glasses on and turned to see JR standing next to Elbee. Once her eyes finally focused, she began to smile. She was finally getting to meet him in person.

"So I finally get to meet my grandbaby in person. After all these years, he's here," she said, giving JR a hug.

"How do you know this is your grandson, Ma?" Elbee asked in amazement.

"I knew that baby was my grandson when I saw him on the news three years ago. They interviewed him after he hit the shot that won his team the AAU regional tournament. When I looked in his face, I knew he could only be your child."

She walked over to her coffee table, pulled out a scrapbook, and looked at JR. "Ever since I saw you that day, I have been keeping track of you. I wanted to contact you, but I didn't know who your mother was and I didn't want to seem like a crazy lady."

"Ma, I don't know if you remember the girl that I was with all summer after I graduated named Saundra Thompson."

"Yeah, I remember her. She was the most precious thing. She came around a lot for the first few months after you went to the military, and then she just stopped. I always wondered what happened to her. I just knew she was gonna be my daughter-in-law."

"Well, Ma, that's JR's mother. But, Ma, if you knew I had a son, why didn't you say something?"

JR sat next to his grandmother on the couch and began looking through the scrapbook. She had every article that had been written about him since his AAU win.

Barbara looked at her son. "I did tell you. Do you remember me asking you did you have a son because I saw a little boy on

TV that looked like you?"

"Yeah. So?"

"That was my way of telling you," she said, smiling.

"Ma, that ain't telling me nothing. Plus, how could you be so sure he was my son?",Elbee asked, still harassing his mother.

"Because he looked just like you did when you were his age. He also has the big nose, big ears, and those soup-cooler lips really confirmed it for me."

Folding his lips in, JR said, "Grandma, go 'head with the lip jokes please."

Hugging on her grandson, she replied, "Don't worry, baby. Your daddy and cousins have those lips, too."

Elbee walked over and started kissing and licking on his mother's face. "That's right. They're big, but they're better to kiss you with my dear."

"Stop playin', boy!" she snapped. "Let me spend some time with my grandson."

Elbee sat on the couch watching as the most important woman in his life and his son interacted like they had known each other for years. Excited as Mom Dukes was to have a grandson, he knew it was time to tell his wife-to-be. How was she going to take the news? Now that was the question.

100 Points

Elbee signed his last bonus check and leaned back in his chair. He couldn't believe that even after getting to the office at seven o'clock in the morning, he was still there at six that evening. In the last year, he had really come to understand what his grandparents were talking about when they said they worked from can't see to can't see. Over the past twelve months, he had been working from can't see in the morning 'til can't see at night.

He was putting the recommendations in an inner office envelope, when his phone began to ring.

"Beltek Technologies, Elbee speaking."

"Hey, Elbee, what you up to?" the caller asked.

"Finishing up some work. Who's dis, JR?"

"Yeah. Are you coming to my game tonight?"

"First things first. The question is what are you up to. Practice speaking correct English so when it's time for you to be interviewed you won't sound crazy. Secondly, sure I'll be there. As a matter of fact, I have to pick up your cousin Benny from the Mercedes dealership, so I'll bring him, too."

"Okay. I'll tell Mom to get tickets for you guys. I called Grandma already, and she said she was coming, too. I'm gonna score a hundred points tonight."

"Nigga, please," Elbee said, laughing. "Your sorry ass ain't gonna break my scoring record."

"Yeah, I heard about you and Cousin Benny both putting up fifty-five points in a game and holding scoring records. Just watch what I do tonight."

"Yeah, yeah, yeah, little punk. You just play your game and the points will come."

"I hear you. Okay, I gotta go. I'll see you at the game, Pops."

"Aw'ight, dude, I'll see you there."

Elbee hung up the phone and decided to bask in the thought of his son doing what he had missed out on. He felt sadness over the fact that he had just met his son, but he promised himself that he would make the best of the rest of the time they would share.

Elbee dropped the recommendations in his box, completing all of his tasks. With that done, he was going to be able to focus more on what he needed to do for the wedding. The nine months since he had proposed to Angel had moved quickly. He loved Angel, but with the reemergence of Saundra and his newfound son, his mind was filled with a bunch of 'what if' questions.

Elbee picked up the phone and dialed Angel. The phone rang four times before she picked up.

"Hello."

"Hey, sweetie."

Speak Now Or...Hold Your Piece

"Hey, Elbee. What are you still doing at the office?"

"Just finishing up the bonus recommendations so I can concentrate solely on the wedding next week."

"That's good, because you haven't been worth a damn concerning the wedding so far," Angel said, laughing.

"What do you mean? I have helped out a lot. As a matter of fact, I did the hardest part."

"And what was that?" she asked, sounding sarcastic.

"I bought the ring. Without that, there wouldn't even be a wedding."

"You have a very twisted way of looking at things," Angel replied, laughing. "Enough about that. What are we doing tonight?"

"Well, I gotta pick Benny up from the dealership and make a stop. Then we can do dinner, if that's okay."

"Sure, sweetie, that will be fine."

"Okay. Pick the restaurant and I'll meet you there. Plus, I need to talk to you about something."

"That's fine, baby. I'll see you later."

Elbee got off the phone and grabbed his bag. Tonight was going to be a pivotal night in his life.

Surprise Surprise

Since Elbee was going to be late, Angel decided to sit on the couch and relax. She picked up the remote, channel surfing until she came across an old episode of *Martin*. Just as she started to get comfortable, the telephone rang.

"Hello."

"Hi, baby."

"Hey, Momma," Angel responded with excitement. "What are you and Dad up to? I can't wait for you guys to get here Thursday."

"Well, baby, you don't have to wait until then."

"What's going on, Ma?" Angel asked inquisitively.

"I convinced your father that we should fly instead of catching the bus."

"That's good. So when do you want to leave and go back so I can purchase your tickets?"

"Girl, you have a wedding to pay for. Plus, your father has plenty of money...the old miser."

Angel laughed at her mother because she was speaking the truth. Her father could definitely squeeze on a dollar until the eagle grinned, as Chuck Brown would say.

"So when will you be in town?"

"Surprise, surprise, surprise! We will be landing at Reagan National Airport at nine-thirty tonight."

"What? Ma, it's seven o'clock now."

"Yeah, I know. We're at the airport now. We're coming in on AirTran Airways, flight 1221. Okay, sweetie, I gotta go. They're calling for us to board our flight now. See you in about two and a half hours."

"Okay. See you in a little bit, Ma."

"Oh and, Angel, your father said make sure Elbee is around. Love you."

When Angel heard the phone go dead, she got up from the couch. She looked at her house and decided she needed to tidy up a little bit. *I finally get to surprise Elbee,* she thought. *I won't tell him anything. I'll just have him meet them when he gets to the restaurant. Whatever he needs to talk to me about can wait until later.*

"This is so perfect," Angel mumbled as she went to take a shower.

What Did Angel Say

Elbee pulled into the parking lot of the Mercedes Benz dealership and scanned the parking lot for Benny. He was about to get out of his truck, when he noticed Benny leaning against a red Honda Accord. Elbee beeped the horn twice to get his attention.

Benny looked up and raised his hand, signaling for Elbee to give him a minute. Elbee pulled the CD cartridge from underneath the seat and changed the CDs. He had reloaded the CD changer when he looked up and saw that Benny was still talking to the lady in the Honda.

Elbee hit the horn again. "Come on, fool. I got somewhere to be," he yelled out of the window.

Benny walked over to the truck. "Why are you rushing a brotha? Hell, Angel ain't goin' nowhere. I was tryin' to get my mack on."

"Whatever, punk. I know Angel ain't goin' nowhere. I'm tryin' not to be late for JR's game."

"And when you say JR, you're talkin' 'bout the youngin'

Speak Now Or...Hold Your Piece

from the gym?"

"Yeah, JR...my son."

"When did all this come about?"

"You remember Saundra Thompson that went to school with us, right?"

"Hell yeah, I remember Saundra. Everybody wanted to tap dat ass back in the day. After seeing how fine she is now, I still want to hit that. That's not her son. Nigga, you ain't get none of that, so stop lyin' on your dick. You know what happens when you lie on your dick."

"We hooked up the night before I left for basic training and she got pregnant."

"Dawg, how you gonna have a son all these years and not tell me? Better yet, how you gonna have a son and not take care of him?"

"Because I didn't know I had a son until a month and a half ago."

"What the fuck!"

"I know, dawg. When I left for basic training, we were writing each other. Then, all of a sudden, I stopped getting letters from her. I kept writing her until the letters started coming back to me."

"So you run into her last month and she dropped this shit on you? That's crazy as hell. Are you sure the kid is yours? She ain't tryin' to Billie Jean you, is she?"

"Billie Jean me? What?"

"She ain't your lover and the kid ain't your son."

"He looks just like me."

"Nigga, I look like you and you ain't my daddy. Are you?"

"You're stupid as hell, you know that? But, I'm sure

211

because we did a DNA test."

"So what did Angel say when you told her?"

"I haven't told her yet," Elbee mumbled.

"Dude! So when are you gonna tell her? After y'all married and Saundra wants child support?"

"She don't want child support, and I'm gonna tell her at dinner tonight."

"Well, if that's the case, stop driving like you driving Ms. Daisy so I can see my lil' cousin bust some bama asses."

Night Night

Tasha watched as Rocky's face became contorted while he climaxed. Having sex with Rocky was better than what she had been getting since Elbee left her, but it wasn't mind blowing. As she climbed from on top of Rocky, she immediately began regretting sleeping with him. Rocky was lying next to Tasha pulling off his condom.

"Damn, girl, you got skills. I don't see how dude would leave you to be with my wife. She sucks in bed."

"Well, if that's the case, why do you still want her?" Tasha shot back, while thinking he wasn't the greatest in bed either.

In a stern tone, Rocky replied, "That's my business, and you need not be asking me about my business."

"I don't know who the hell you're used to dealing with, but I promise you that I ain't them. So just like you ask me questions about my business, I'm gonna ask you questions. If you don't like that, you can try dealing with Elbee yourself and let me know how that works for you."

Before Rocky could reply, his cell phone rang. As he

listened to the caller, a sinister smile formed on his face. When he ended his call, he was elated.

"What you so happy about?" Tasha snapped.

Rocky got up from the bed and started putting his clothes on. He looked Tasha in her eyes and said, "I'm happy because I just got the information I need to put an end to the wedding."

"And what is that? 'Cause I know Elbee didn't get caught cheating."

Visually upset, Rocky snapped, "Why do people around here treat that nigga like he's a god or something? He ain't shit!" he yelled. "Nothing! A nobody!"

"People like Elbee because he's charming and charismatic. But, most of all, he has a good heart and gives back to the neighborhood."

"Yeah, well, fuck that shit. People ain't gonna think so highly of his bitch ass when they find out he has a fifteen-year-old son that he ain't taking care of," Rocky stated matter-of-factly.

Tasha's mouth fell open. She couldn't believe what she had just heard. *This can't be true. Elbee would never abandon his child,* she thought. "Are you sure about your information?" Tasha asked, still astonished by this new revelation.

"My people are always 100% sure about information before they give it to me. So, with this new info, I don't need your stankin' ass anymore." Rocky turned and pointed his gun at Tasha. "Night night," he said right before pulling the trigger.

Rocky wiped his fingerprints off the gun, tossed it on the bed, and grabbed the trash bag out of the trash can. Then he headed out to meet Tony.

"I love it when a plan comes together."

Number 28

You would have thought Elbee and Benny were superstars when they walked through the door of the gym, with both of them sporting DeMarco Solar sweat suits. Everybody was jockeying for position to shake their hands or speak to them. It had been like that since they were teenagers in high school. With both of them making the All Metropolitan basketball team and playing in the McDonald's Classic, everyone knew who they were.

"I see ya'll still bring a crowd."

Elbee and Benny turned around to see their old coach standing there in a black We R One sweat suit. Coach Bailey stood 6'6" tall with a chocolate complexion. He had played one season with the Washington Bullets before blowing out his knee. With his basketball career over, he started teaching and coaching basketball at Suitland High School. Under his leadership, the Rams had won five state titles. Two titles with Benny, two more with Benny and Elbee together, and one with JR.

"Yeah, and we can see you still winning," Benny replied, giving Coach Bailey a hug. Benny looked down at his sweat suit. "I see you still visit the We R One store on a regular."

"Well, you know your boy who owns the store knows how to take care of a brotha. What up, Elbee?"

"What's going on, Coach? How you be?"

"I'm good. Hoping I bring another title to the school before I retire."

"Well, from what I hear, that's about to happen."

"I got a real good chance, El. I just gotta get my point guard under control. He plays just like you use to, with attitude and all."

"I wonder why?" Benny mumbled.

"Shut up, Benny."

"Now, Elbee, I know we haven't talked in a while, but I could use your help with him."

"Are you talking about JR?"

"Yeah, how did you know?" the coach asked, amazed.

"I've played him a few times. He has my mouth and Benny's temper," Elbee said, looking at Benny.

"Can we keep talking about JR and not me," Benny chimed in.

"We'll talk more after the game. Okay, fellas?" Coach Bailey said before heading over to the bench.

Elbee looked around the gym. "There's Saundra over there. Let's go grab a seat."

"Damn, Saundra is fine as frog hairs."

Elbee shot Benny an elbow. "That's my baby's mama, fool."

"Well, I think I need to be his big cousin and step daddy

since you getting married in a few."

"You is straight ignant," Elbee replied, shaking his head. "Hey, Saundra, how you doing?"

"Elbee, how did you get in? I was waiting for you to call so I could bring you these tickets."

"He came with me and you know how I do," Benny interjected.

"Hi, Benjamin," Saundra said in a singsong type of way.

"After all these years, you still know how to make my name sound good," Benny responded, giving her a hug. "Girl, you know I still wanna marry you."

"That would be fine, Benjamin, but I'm in love with someone else," she replied as she looked at Elbee. "So, I wouldn't want us to get married and I can't get him off my mind. I did that already, and it didn't work out too well."

"I hear you. So where's my lil' cousin at?"

"He's the one wearing number twenty-eight," Saundra answered, still eyeballing Elbee.

"Why is he wearing that number? He should be wearing number thirty-three like his big cousin."

"Well, Benjamin, his father wore the number twenty-eight when he played basketball."

"Yeah, yeah, yeah. I see my aunt. I'm going to sit with her."

The color guard came and did the Star Spangled Banner. Then the game began. As Elbee sat watching the game, he thought about what had transpired. He just hoped getting to know his son wasn't going to jeopardize his relationship, because he wasn't going to miss out on anymore of his son's life.

Just Being a Man

Elbee was on cloud nine as he drove to the Fish Market Restaurant in Clinton, Maryland It was exciting for him to watch his son put Suitland's basketball team on his back and carry them to victory. What made it even better was that JR told the team he was dedicating the win to his dad. That was the first time JR had acknowledged him as his father.

While parking the car, Elbee started getting nervous about telling Angel that he had a fifteen-year-old son. He didn't have a clue on how she would take the news. That's why it was taking him so long to tell her. He hoped she would understand. If she didn't, C'est las vie. It is what it is.

Elbee walked into the Fish Market prepared for whatever decision Angel made. He felt he had planned perfectly when and where he was going to tell her. By choosing a public place, he guaranteed himself one thing. That was, she wouldn't cause a scene.

At the door scanning the restaurant, Elbee saw Angel standing at the bar talking. He started walking over to her, but

Speak Now Or...Hold Your Piece

midstride he noticed Angel laughing with the gentleman and touch him in a way of affection. Seeing this brought back feelings of Tasha cheating. Taking a deep breath, he decided not to jump to any conclusions. So, he continued walking over to where they were.

Standing behind her defensively, he said, "Hey, Angel."

"Hey, honey. You made it," Angel responded, turning to give him a hug. "Would you like a drink or something? Our table isn't ready yet."

As anger began building inside him, all Elbee heard was, "Wah, wah, wah." Although he was not a jealous person, he was not going to be played again, no matter how much he loved Angel.

Looking past Angel, he introduced himself to the gentleman. "Hi, I'm Elbee, Angel's fiancé."

"It's nice to meet you, Elbee. I'm Angel's dad."

Elbee felt all of the wind go out of his sails. The anger began to subside and calmness started to come over him.

Taking a deep breath, Elbee asked the bartender, "Can I get a double shot of 1738?"

Mr. Terry began to laugh.

"What's so funny, Dad?" Angel asked. "And what's wrong with you, Elbee?"

"Ahh, baby girl, leave the boy alone. He was just being a man," Mr. Terry replied, shaking his soon-to-be son-in-law's hand. "Elbee here was just making sure I wasn't tryin' to move in on his woman. I recognized him when he came in the door from the pictures you emailed your mother."

"Please forgive me, Mr. Terry," Elbee begged, taking a sip of his drink.

219

"No need to apologize, son. I would have done the same thing."

"And who is this handsome gentleman? This must be my new son-in-law," Mrs. Terry commented, giving Elbee a hug.

"Yes, Mama, this is Elbee."

At that moment, the hostess came over and let Angel know that their table was ready.

As they started walking over to the table, Elbee whispered, "I thought they were coming in town the week before the wedding. They're three weeks early."

"I know. They called after you did to say they were at the airport getting on a plane to come here."

"Okay, well, I need some alone time with you."

"That's fine, baby."

"So I guess this means no punanny tonight, huh?"

"You guessed right."

"That's some fraggle naggle bull. It's okay, though. I'll just hang out with my girl Betty. She's always got me."

"And who is Betty? Don't make me hurt you, Elbee."

"You know Betty…Betty Palm and her four sisters," Elbee joked.

"You're stupid."

Dad

JR was in the passenger seat relaxing as his mother drove to the restaurant. His mind was burning with questions as the mellow sounds of Sylver Logan Sharp blared through the Bose speakers of the Lexus. How could he ask his mother the questions he wanted answers to without her getting upset?

"What's up, son? You're awfully quiet for a person who just had twenty-five points, fifteen assists, and ten steals in a winning effort."

"Nothing, Ma, I'm fine."

"Usually when people say there isn't anything wrong, it usually is. Plus, I know my son very well, and the only time he isn't harassing me to hear TCB, CCB or any of them other alphabet bands is after a loss. So what's up?"

JR sat for a second wondering if he should open up this can of worms. He didn't want to offend his mother because she had sacrificed so much for him.

"Baby, you can talk to me about anything."

"Even about Dad?" JR asked sheepishly.

"Especially about your dad."

"Well, Grandma says she remembers when you were going to Suitland with Dad."

"Okay," she said, knowing where JR was about to go with the question.

"And she has been living in the same house since then. So I guess I wanna know what happened between you and Dad that kept him from seeing me all these years."

"JR, nothing happened. Your dad left to go into the military and didn't know I was pregnant. Your father was also young and hotheaded like you are now. I was afraid if he knew I was pregnant that he might have gone AWOL to be home with me. Then, by the time I was ready to tell him, I had met your stepfather and we were getting married. He asked could he adopt you, and I said yeah until I found out Elbee would have to sign the papers to make it legal. Telling him that way would have caused even more problems."

"So what type of guy was Dad growing up?" JR asked, looking at his mother.

After parking the car, Saundra leaned back in her seat and paused with a twinkle in her eye. "Your father was a handsome, charismatic, flirtatious clown."

"Clown?" JR replied curiously.

"Yes, a clown. As you get to know him, you will see that he always seems to be on joke time, but through all of his playing, the girls all loved him. I just never understood why I was the one he wanted."

"Mom, did you love him?"

"I have always loved your father. He was the first man I

ever loved."

"So why haven't you told him?" JR responded as they walked into the restaurant.

Saundra stood looking at her son as he walked up to the hostess, thinking to herself, *I wish it was that easy. If he only knew how many times I thought about telling Elbee how I felt, only to find out he was still just chasing women.*

Walking towards his mother, JR said, "Ma, you should have told him. Oh and don't tell me that it's not that easy, because you don't let me use that excuse. What is it that you always tell me? Let me see. Hmmm. Oh yeah, you won't know how things will turn out until you tell a person."

Saundra stood looking at her son and shaking her head. She hated when he used the things she taught him against her. If she didn't know anything else, she knew Elbee Elton Thompson was definitely his father's child. Being born a day apart didn't help matters.

JR gave his mother a hug. "I'm gonna go holla at the fellas for a minute. While I'm gone, think about what I just said. Love you."

The News

Rocky was anxious to get somewhere and get settled. The only problem was that Tony wasn't going anywhere near the hotel. Rocky really wanted to be somewhere, anywhere, so he could see the news. This last ditch effort to break up Elbee and Angel had cost him a pretty penny and some favors, but he felt if it worked, it would all be worth it.

"Tony, where the hell are we going?"

"Just chill, Rock. I got you."

"Man, I need to see the news."

"And you will, nigga. Just chill. Damn!"

"Dude, you keep sayin' that, but your punk ass ain't nowhere near the hotel. So what's up?"

"Well, nigga, if you hadn't killed the Tasha broad, we could've went back to the hotel."

"What does she have to do with anything?" Rocky replied, frustrated.

"How about the fact that her body was found, her face is

Speak Now Or...Hold Your Piece

being plastered over the TV, and the hotel has you on video going back to the room with her."

"Damn! How did you find out?"

"The hoodrat cleanin' broad tipped me off. I hit her off with a grand to say see hadn't seen us again. Rock, this shit with Angel is gettin' costly and a lil' outta hand."

"Fuck dat, Tony! I don't wanna hear that shit! I'm gettin' my wife back, and no one is gonna stop me! So, if you ain't wit' me, take your ass on somewhere!" Rocky yelled.

"Rock, I'm wit' you, but I also don't wanna go broke or to jail behind some bitch that I ain't fuckin'," Tony shot back.

"My bad. I got you, Tone. So where are we going now?"

"To the last place they would think to look for us."

Tony pulled up and parked a block away from Elbee's building.

"Why are we over by this fool's house?"

Tony smiled and grabbed his beard. "Do you remember the lil' bun-bun that I told you that I met? Well, her sister lives in one of the units and works at night, so she keeps her kids."

"My man! So we can keep an eye on that nigga."

"And you know this, mannnnnnn."

Tony and Rocky had gotten out of the car and was starting to walk up the street, when a black Lexus passed by. Rocky didn't pay it any attention and kept walking until Tony stopped him.

"Slow your roll, Rock. That's Angel."

Rocky was in awe when he saw Angel step out of the car. She was even more beautiful than he had remembered. Her caramel brown complexion glowed in the reflection of the moonlight. Her eyes sparkled like the North Star and her succulent lips accentuated her smile. Her butt was voluptuous and her breast added to her sexiness. She looked simply ethereal.

Damn, he thought. *How could I have treated her the way I did? Things are going to be different this time around. Once I get her back, I'm going to treat her like the queen that she is.*

Rocky was brought back to reality when Elbee opened the door and Angel immediately started kissing on his bare chest. He just stared as Angel dropped to her knees and began giving Elbee oral gratification before his door fully closed. Tony looked at Rocky, saw the fire in his eyes, and grabbed him before he could do anything crazy.

"Just hold on a little longer, Rock, and his bitch ass will be outta the picture."

"Yeah, you're right. Let's get in here and check out this newscast."

Is He or Isn't He

Elbee leaned back in his seat and took a deep breath. The time had finally come for him to tell Angel about JR. He had expected to tell her three weeks ago, but her parents came into town early and threw a monkey wrench in his plans.

Then it seemed that every time he tried to tell her for some strange reason something came up or somebody came around. The wedding day was quickly approaching. Therefore, it was a must that he tell her. Plus, he had added JR and Saundra to the wedding list. So, he wanted her to know before she started asking questions.

Elbee was flipping through channels, when his cell phone rang. When he looked, he saw it was Angel and picked up quickly.

"Holla at your boy."

"Hey, sweetie, what are you doing?"

"Just flipping through channels and waiting for you to get here. By the way, what are you wearing?" Elbee asked seductively.

"I'm wearing those Levis that you like so much and the shirt that you bought me from DeMarco. But, honey, I might not be able to stop by tonight."

"Come on, boo. You done had a brotha on PR ever since your folks got here. I need to at least smell the punanny. Damn," Elbee whined.

"But I have to pick up my mother from the salon," Angel chuckled.

"She'll be alright at the salon with Shanté. Hell, call Shanté and have your mother get a full body massage. I'll pay for it."

"No, boy, we still have a lot of stuff to do."

"Angel, Betty and her four sistas need a break."

"I don't know, baby."

Elbee heard the doorbell ring. "Hold on, sweetie. Somebody's at the door."

Elbee opened the door to see Angel standing there, and immediately his nature started to rise.

Angel looked down at Elbee's shorts. "Are those your keys or is someone happy to see me?"

She gave Elbee a passionate kiss and dropped to her knees to begin giving Elbee oral gratification before his door could be fully closed. Elbee tried to gather himself and keep from knocking down his lamp as he enjoyed the pleasure being given to him. It had been almost a month since he and Angel had been intimate, and he was going to enjoy every minute of it.

Angel saw that her man loved every lick she gave his magic stick. She liked pleasing him, especially since he did so much to please her. Elbee was getting ready to climax when he stopped her.

Speak Now Or...Hold Your Piece

"Your turn, baby. It's time for me to smell the punanny."

Elbee was turned on even more when he undressed Angel and saw one of the sexiest bra and panty sets she had ever worn. It had taken some time, but Elbee had finally gotten Angel to only wear matching bra and panty sets for times just like these. He knelt over her marveling at her beauty.

Elbee had just started licking Angel's thighs, when the news reporter on TV said that Tasha Butler had just been found murdered in her home.

"Elbee, did you hear that?"

"Hear what?" Elbee asked, while still trying to lick on Angels' thighs.

"Tasha was found murdered."

"Okay, we'll send flowers," Elbee mumbled, still trying to get his freak on.

"Elbee!" Angel exclaimed. "Listen to the news."

Elbee and Angel got off the floor and sat on the couch. The reporter stated that Tasha was found in her townhouse after being dead for three weeks. She had been reported missing by some of her co-workers after she hadn't been heard from. The reports were that when the police entered her home, they found her naked in her bed and dead. The cause of death was a broken neck.

Both Elbee and Angel were stunned by the news. They both wanted Tasha out of their lives, but not like this. How could something like this have happened? This new revelation brought Elbee back to his senses, and he realized now was the time to tell Angel about JR.

"Angel, I have to tell you something important," Elbee mumbled.

As soon as Elbee started to speak, the sports segment of the news came on.

"Angel, I—"

"Wait a minute, Elbee. I got a text telling me to watch the sports tonight."

"Tonight, we would like to introduce everyone to our local athlete of the week, Elbee Elton Thompson, but everyone calls him JR," the newscaster announced.

Angel looked at Elbee with anger and disdain as her eyes filled with tears. She felt like she was in the twilight zone. This couldn't be happening.

"Okay, let me explain," Elbee said in a calm voice.

"There is nothing to explain, unless that's your son. Is that your son?"

"It's not that easy," he stammered.

"What do you mean it's not that easy? Is he or is he not your son? How fuckin' hard of a question is that?"

"Angel, it's not that cut and dry."

"Elbee, either he's your son or he isn't. That's all I'm asking you. Yes or no?" Angel questioned in a stern voice.

"Yes, he is," Elbee answered, "but let me explain."

"There's nothing for you to explain, you lying bastard. I can't believe I trusted you. You disgust me, and by the way, the wedding is off!"

Angel finished putting her clothes on, grabbed her coat, and stormed out the door.

This is not how it was supposed to happen. I was supposed to get a chance to tell her before she could find out. Then I would have had a chance to explain, Elbee thought.

Tasha is dead and still causing problems. No one else could have sent that text, Elbee thought to himself. *No, it couldn't have been Tasha. She's been dead for three weeks according to the news. Something isn't right. Someone is out to get me. Damn!*

Wedding is Off

The knock at her room door brought Angel out of her trance. She had been in her bedroom ever since she had come in the house the night before. She felt so betrayed by Elbee. How could he have a fifteen-year-old son and not tell her about him? More importantly, what type of man was Elbee not taking care of his son?

Her bedroom door opened up, and Rhonda and Carolyn stuck their heads in the room.

"Hey, honey, how are you?" Carolyn asked.

"I'm doing good, I guess," Angel replied.

"Well, Aunt Theresa seems to think you're upset about something," Carolyn continued.

"I wonder what would make her think that," Angel responded sarcastically.

"Oh, I don't know. Probably the fact that you told her the wedding was called off."

When Carolyn mentioned the wedding, Angel started crying. The more she thought about it, the more hurt she felt. Of

Speak Now Or...Hold Your Piece

all the people in the world, she never thought Elbee would hurt her like this.

"I called off the wedding because Elbee is a lying dog, and he has been lying to me the entire time we've been together."

"About what, sweetie? What could be so bad that you called off the wedding?" Rhonda asked.

"I found out Elbee has a fifteen-year-old son that he never told me about," Angel snapped.

"What?" Carolyn said, startled.

"He has a fifteen-year-old son that he hasn't been taking care of," Angel blurted out.

"Oh my God, I can't believe that," Carolyn said in disbelief.

"It's not what you think," Rhonda interjected.

"Excuse me! You knew about this?" Angel questioned.

"Yes, I knew about JR, but it's not what you're thinking," Rhonda answered. "Elbee—"

Angel cut Rhonda off. "Get the fuck outta my house, you bitch!" she yelled.

"Angel!" Carolyn snapped.

"Angel my ass! She was supposed to be my friend, and now I see that she's just as big a liar as Elbee! Now get the fuck out of my house, Rhonda!" Angel continued to shout.

"I am your friend, Angel, and I'm sorry you feel the way that you do," Rhonda replied as she headed out the door.

Carolyn followed Rhonda into the living room. As Rhonda was reaching for her coat, Carolyn stopped her.

"Rhonda, don't leave."

"I don't want to upset Angel anymore than she already is."

"Let me worry about that. Have a seat while I speak to Angel for a moment. I'm sure she'll be happy to let you explain when I'm done. Hell, I wanna know what's going on myself," Carolyn said as both of them laughed.

Carolyn walked back into the room where Angel was. She could see Angel was physically shaken. Whatever was going on was tearing her apart.

"Angel, what's wrong with you? Why would you talk to Rhonda like that? She's your friend."

"She's not my friend. If she was truly my friend, she wouldn't have kept Elbee's lies and secrets for him."

"What did Elbee lie about?" Carolyn asked, still very much confused.

"He has a fifteen-year-old son that he never told me about."

"Well, did he say why he didn't tell you about his son?"

"I didn't let him because I didn't want to hear anymore of his lies."

"Angel, I'm your cousin and I love you dearly. So, don't get mad when I say this, but have you told him about your marriage?"

When Carolyn said that, Angel looked at her with teary eyes.

"Why would you say that to me? You know I have a reason for not telling him about that."

"And maybe he has a reason for not telling you about his son. If it's good for you, then it should be good for him, too."

"Yeah, but Rhonda should have said something."

"You mean like Blak should have said something to his boy that he grew with most of his life? Think about that, and then come apologize to Rhonda."

Carolyn walked out of the room and left Angel to her thoughts. The whole time she had been upset with Elbee, she didn't even begin to think about what she was keeping from him. Things she would never tell him.

Secrets

Elbee couldn't believe what happened. *Of all the times for JR to be player of the week, it would have to be this week,* he thought to himself. Elbee started to feel the regret of not forcing the issue and telling Angel about JR right away.

What was he going to do now? How was he going to tell his mother? She had already promised to get rid of him and keep Angel if he screwed up. This was a mistake of major proportion.

As he sat going through a series of questions, Elbee began to get angry.

I didn't even know about JR, he thought. *If she had been spending some time with me, she would have known. Fuck her! That's my son, and I'm gonna be a father to him,* he concluded.

"What up, yo?" Blak exclaimed as he burst into Elbee's home.

"Nigga, what the hell happened to knockin'? Damn!"

"Do you knock on my door when you come to my house?"

Elbee looked at Blak. "No, fool, because I got a damn key."

Speak Now Or... Hold Your Piece

"Right and I have the key to yours, punk."

They both laughed as Blak plopped down on the couch.

"You got one more week before you walk the green mile. Are you ready?" Blak asked.

"Ready for what? I hope you ain't talking 'bout that bullshit-ass wedding. 'Cause if you are, don't worry about it. Angel called it off."

Blak looked at Elbee and could see the pain and disappointment in his face. "What do you mean she called it off?"

"What does 'she called it off' mean, fool? Don't you have a college education?"

"Yeah, nigga. Fuck you. So what you do?"

"Nothing. She found out about JR," Elbee replied, dropping his head.

"She found out about JR! All this time you've been working out with JR and you hadn't told her? What the fuck, Elbee!"

"Dawg, I've been trying to tell her for weeks. Her parents coming to town early hasn't left us with a lot of time alone. Fool, I done beat my meat so much in the past few weeks that I just bought stock in Nivea lotion."

"Damn, dude! That's what I would call irreconcilable differences," Blak said, laughing. "Well, if you didn't tell her, who did?"

"What had happened was Angel came over last night wearing a rain jacket."

"But, dawg, it wasn't raining last night."

"I know," Elbee replied, looking at Blak with his eyes stretched. "She had on a *rain coat*," he said again, putting emphasis on the last two words.

"I heard you say she had on a—" At that point, it was like a light went off in Blak's head. "Oh, ohhhhhh...she had on a rain coat. Now I see."

"Rightttttt. My intention was to tell her as soon as she got here. But, she opened up her coat and my dick got harder than Chinese arithmetic being done by a Russian in the dark under water. Then she dropped to her knees and kissed Elbee Jr., and it was on like popcorn."

"T.M.I., dude, T.M.I. So from there, how did she find out?"

"I'm getting to that now. So while we were getting our freak on, she stopped me so she could hear the story about Tasha getting killed."

Blak interrupted. "Did you say Tasha was murdered?"

"Yep, that's what I said."

"Damn, that's fucked up. Have you talked to her parents yet?"

"Not yet, but I'm gonna call them later," Elbee replied, shaking his head. "Let me finish telling you what happened. So immediately after that story went off, they went into sports, and who was the top story?"

"JR. Wowwwww. But did you tell her that you just found out about JR?"

"No, Blak, I didn't get to tell her that. Fadoop fadoop."

"Fuck you, Elbee!"

"I tried to tell her, but she refused to let me explain. Then she kept calling me a liar and told me to get out of her house."

Blak was shocked. He couldn't believe Angel would say something like that, especially after she begged him to keep her secret.

"I tell you what. The fellas got your bachelor party planned for tonight. You just be ready when I get back. Hell, if it turns out not to be a bachelor party, you can just do what Beyoncé said and put your freakum clothes on. Then we'll party with some women who will be buckey naked."

Elbee started laughing. "Cool beans."

Blak dapped Elbee up and headed out the door. It was time he reminded Angel that she had some secrets of her own.

Don't Go Away Mad Just Go Away

The gym was pretty empty when Elbee walked in. Blak wasn't going to pick him up for at least another four hours, so he decided to shoot some ball to relax his mind. Elbee walked past the young lady at the desk and grabbed a ball.

He had been shooting around by himself for about twenty minutes before someone came over.

"Hey, can we shoot with you?" a tall, dark complexioned man asked.

"Sure, why not?" Elbee responded.

Elbee played a game of thirty-three with the two gentlemen for about fifteen minutes. He looked at the game as just some time to shoot around, although he had noticed the two gentlemen were playing really hard.

"Ahh thirty-three!" the stranger barked. "You're not as good as everyone says you are."

Speak Now Or...Hold Your Piece

"Excuse me? What did you say, slim?" Elbee asked inquisitively.

"I said you're not as good as people say you are."

Elbee just shook his head and started to walk away. With everything he was going through, he wasn't going to go at it with this bum.

"That's right. Walk away before I have to show everyone that you really can't ball."

Elbee stopped and looked the dude in the eyes. "Slim, if you only knew."

"Come on, man, let's go," the other stranger said.

"Naw, Tony, I just beat this chump in thirty-three, and I got a thousand dollars that says I can beat him one on one."

"Okay, slim. One on one for a one thousand dollar bet with an extra hundred dollars for each point I beat you by."

The stranger looked at Elbee and snarled, "Let's do it. Where's your money, punk?"

Elbee looked at the gym owner. "You got me, Danté?"

"Yeah, I got you, El," he replied.

The stranger threw the ball into Elbee's chest. "Check ball, nigga!"

When word got around the gym that Elbee was playing someone for money, a crowd started to gather around the court.

"Are you sure you wanna give me the ball first?"

"Yeah, it's your court, so it's your ball."

"Well, if that's the case," Elbee shot the ball and hit nothing but net, "that's one."

Elbee hit three more jumpers, making the score four to zero.

"I'm not as good as people say I am? Take this," he said as he hit another jumper.

"Nigga, you ain't got nuthin' but that jumper," the stranger barked.

Elbee started dribbling the ball as the crowd grew larger. When he went to his right, the stranger was right there. Then Elbee went left, only to find the stranger right there with him.

"See? I told you," the stranger snarled.

Elbee drove hard left to the basket, crossed over to his right hand, and layed the ball up off the glass.

Elbee walked back to the foul line shaking his head. "Compliments of Mr. Iverson."

Next, Elbee backed the stranger down towards the basket. Once he got him into the post, he faked left and went right, laying the ball up with his left hand.

"You can thank Hakeem the Dream for that one," Elbee taunted.

The next shot was a fade away jumper.

"Oooooh, fade away MJ," Elbee sang, laughing. "That's seven to nuthin', homeboy."

The people in the stands were oohing and aahing as Elbee was clowning and scoring at the same time. The stranger had truly pissed him off, and he was going to make him look bad for it.

During the course of Elbee playing around, the stranger stole the ball and went racing towards the basket. Just as he went to lay the ball up, Elbee came out of nowhere and blocked his shot.

"Get that shit outta here!" Elbee yelled, grabbing the ball before it went out of bounds.

"My ball!" the stranger exclaimed.

"Your ball? Nigga, please!" Elbee shot back.

"You fouled me."

"Fouled you? Nigga, please!"

"It's my ball."

"Okay," Elbee said, tossing him the ball. "The score is twelve to nuthin', and for that bullshit, I promise you that you won't score. You can bet on that."

"I will. How 'bout another grand, punk?"

"It's a bet."

You could hear the guys in the gym bleachers making side bets. "I got five hundred on Elbee," some said, while other guys responded, "I'll take that bet." A lot of money was riding on the next four points.

The stranger started dribbling the ball from right to left. Elbee studied his motion as he anticipated the stranger's move. He was not going to score one point. Not if Elbee had anything to do with it.

With the ball in his left hand, the stranger tried to switch the ball to his right hand. As he tried to make the switch, Elbee timed his movement, stuck his hand out, and stole the ball.

"Gimme that," Elbee said as he took the ball. "It's D and B time, punk."

From the top of the key, Elbee drove to the basket real hard. The stranger started backpedaling, trying to anticipate Elbee's move. He wasn't prepared for what Elbee was going to do next, though. Elbee stepped inside the paint, leaped towards the basket, and dunked the ball. Then he hung on the rim with his legs spread open in the stranger's face.

The gym erupted with people yelling, "Dick and balls! Dick and balls!"

The stranger was furious. Not only was he losing, but he

had just been dunked on and thoroughly embarrassed. If this had been the NBA, he would have been on a poster.

Elbee scored two more points and yelled, "Point game, punk! Have your flunky get my paper together."

Elbee got the ball and didn't even dribble. He just pulled up and shot a jumper.

"Ball game, nigga! That's forty-five hundred that you owe me, slim. Keep the extra hundred as a tip, chump," Elbee said, laughing.

People all over the gym were passing money back and forth. Those who had bet on Elbee were laughing and collecting their winnings. The ones who lost were fussing and telling Elbee that he could have let dude score at least one point.

Elbee looked at the stranger, and in his Chris Tucker voice, he said, "I won. Give me my money," while still laughing.

The stranger turned to his buddy and asked for the money. His boy counted out the cash and handed it to him. The stranger looked at the money and then threw it in Elbee's face.

Elbee looked at the stranger. "That was so disrespectful, you lil' bitch."

The stranger started stepping towards Elbee in a menacing manner until his boy stopped him. The stranger realized it was not the time or the place. With that, he grabbed his gym bag and stormed out the gym.

Elbee continued laughing as he yelled out, "Don't go away mad. Just go away."

Liar

It took Blak only twenty minutes to get to Angel's home. He was infuriated at how high, mighty, and self-righteous Angel was acting. He had put his friendship with Elbee on the line to keep her secret, and this was how she repaid him? It wasn't going down like that. Not today, not ever.

Trying to contain his anger, Blak knocked on the door. He at least wanted to give Angel a chance to explain herself. He could barely remain still while waiting for someone to answer the door.

Angel's mother answered. "Hello, Kym, or is it Blak these days?" Mrs. Terry said as she smiled and gave Blak a hug.

"Hello, Mrs. Terry. How are you? And it's still Kym," Blak replied sheepishly.

"Kym, I'm glad to see you. Angel is upset about something. Maybe you can find out what it is."

"I'll try, Mrs. Terry. Where is she?"

"She's in her room. Her father, Carolyn, and Rhonda are in the family room."

"Thank you, Mrs. Terry," Blak added as he headed back towards the family room.

When Blak walked into the family room, he saw Mr. Terry telling Rhonda and Carolyn one of his famous stories that Blak loved to hear. Hearing them reminded him of the times he spent with his grandfather.

"How are you doing, Mr. Terry?" Blak asked, interrupting Mr. Terry's story.

"Kym, my boy, how are you?"

"I'm fine, sir," Blak responded as he shook Mr. Terry's hand. "I see you're keeping the ladies entertained."

"Yes, I am. No need to have them looking at the boob tube."

Blak kissed Rhonda on the cheek and hugged her. Then he gave Carolyn a hug.

"I'm glad you're here, baby. You need to talk to Angel," Carolyn urged Blak.

"Oooh, that's right. You are dating my niece."

"Yes, sir, I am," Blak confirmed respectfully.

"I couldn't think of a better man for her. If her parents were still living, they would be very proud."

"I'm glad you feel that way, sir. But, if you will excuse me, I need to speak with Angel for a minute."

Blak walked up the stairs to Angel's room and knocked on the door. When she didn't answer, he pushed the door open and stuck his head in. When he looked in the room, he found Angel on her knees praying. So, he just stood quietly and waited for her to finish.

When Angel stood up, she was startled to see Blak standing by her door. She knew exactly what Blak was there for. He was there to plead to Elbee's case, but she didn't want to hear what

Speak Now Or... Hold Your Piece

he had to say. Besides, there wasn't anything Blak could say to her that would change her mind. To her, Elbee was just another deadbeat dad.

"What's going on, Angel?"

"Blak, I know why you're here, and you might as well save your breath."

"But, Angel, you never let Elbee explain."

"There was nothing to explain. Elbee has a son that he didn't tell me about. More importantly, he isn't taking care of him. Elbee is a liar, period."

"So let me get this straight. Elbee not telling you about JR makes him a liar?"

"Yes, it does, Blak!" Angel stated emphatically.

"Hmm. So I guess that makes you an even bigger liar."

"What? Why would you say something like that to me?"

"Because although you have apparently decided to kill him on the imaginary canvas of your mind, you still haven't told Elbee about your ex-husband, have you? Not only have you not told him, but you got me lying for you to MY BEST FRIEND!" Blak hollered.

Hearing Blak raise his voice, everyone in the house ran into the room. Angel stood by her bed crying as Blak turned to leave.

"What's going on?" Mr. Terry demanded, looking at Blak.

"Well, Mr. Terry, your hypocritical daughter has called off the wedding because Elbee didn't tell her about his son that he just found out about himself. Yet, she hasn't told him that she didn't get divorced from her husband until after he proposed to her. Hell, he still doesn't know she was ever married," Blak retorted.

Angel began to cry even more as everyone turned to look at her. After hearing what Blak had to say, she truly felt like the hypocrite that he had just called her. She never had a chance to think everything through. Her emotions had gotten the best of her.

"Blak, I'm sorry. I let my emotions run wild. Do you think Elbee will forgive me?"

"That's not for me to say. You have to ask Elbee."

"Thank you. I will, and thank you for putting me in check," Angel confessed, giving Blak a hug.

•

L.J.G.

Rocky sat back in the recliner proud of himself. He didn't get a chance to whoop Elbee's ass, but he was more than sure the wedding was off. He heard Angel call Elbee a liar and leave. He was sure it was all over because he knew Angel hated being lied to.

Tony walked into the house with a disturbed look on his face. He wasn't looking forward to giving Rocky the news.

"Tony Tone, what's the deal, homie? Why so glum, chum? We got rid of that busta, and I didn't even have to beat that ass," Rocky bragged, smiling like a cheshire cat.

"Don't get too excited, Rock, because the wedding is back on."

"What the hell do you mean the wedding is back on? I beat him, Tony."

"Apparently not, dawg. I don't know what type of mojo that nigga has or if he is just King Ding-a-ling, but the wedding is back on."

"I can't believe this bullshit!" Rocky yelled as he paced

back and forth across the floor. "Fuck it! I'm just gonna have this muthafucka killed!"

"You can't, Rock. None of our hitters will touch him. It's like I told you before, word on the street is that he's untouchable."

"That's on the streets of DC, not our streets. Get a hitter from home."

"Rock, that's on ours, too. Your father put the word out that if anyone touches this dude, he will have them killed. That's after they watch their family die. I don't know who this dude is or who he knows, but he ain't worth the trouble. L.I.G., baby, L.I.G."

"What the hell does L.I.G. mean, Tony?"

"It means let it go, Rock. One broad and one dude ain't worth the heat that these two will bring down on us."

"Fuck it then. I'll kill him myself," Rock concluded as he sat down in a chair and pulled out his gun. "I will have Angel back, and if I can't, neither will he."

Krude 7 Krew

After everything he had been through, Elbee couldn't believe his wedding day had finally come. It had been two years to the exact day he had committed himself to Angel. As he sat in the parlor waiting for the ceremony to begin, his thoughts immediately went to the scripture that stated, "He who findeth a wife finds a good thing." In his heart, he truly believed he had a good thing.

Elbee sat in deep thought until Blak, DB, and Ramon entered the room.

"Elbee, I just want you to know I have a car with four freaks in it waiting out back if you wanna run," Ramon joked, moving towards the door.

"Man, go 'head with that. Just 'cause your wife was crazy don't try and talk the brotha outta marrying a good woman," DB interjected.

"Hell, at least you don't have to worry about Tasha trying to crash the wedding," Blak blurted out before he had a chance to think.

At that moment, there was a hush over Jerusalem. Elbee dropped his head as he thought about the violent death that Tasha had suffered. He had moved on with his life, but he still had some feelings for her.

"Damn, Blak, will you ever learn what the hell to say outta your mouth? Even I wasn't dumb enough to touch that one," Ramon noted, breaking the silence.

"I don't know how this fool ever became the GM of a Fortune 500 company," DB added.

"My bad, El. I didn't mean to bring that up today," Blak sympathized.

"It's cool, Blak. I expect dumb stuff like that from you," Elbee laughed. "Fellas, show me love."

The guys all huddled together and hugged like Martin, Tommy, and Cole would do on *Martin,* and then they started laughing.

The wedding coordinator stuck her head in the room, interrupting their brotherly moment. "It's time."

"Let's do this, fellas," Elbee said nervously.

"Don't worry, brotha. We got your back," DB assured him. "K7K, baby boy."

"It's plain to see you can't change me. I'mma be KRUDE for life," they all said in unison.

Speak Now...

It was a beautiful and unseasonably warm day for Angel and Elbee's wedding. As people pulled up in front of the LonnieBell Mansion, they were amazed at how lovely and elegant it was. This was sure to be a wonderful affair.

The wedding coordinator got everyone seated, and the ceremony began at one o'clock on the dot. Right on cue, the singer started singing *When We Get Married* by Larry Graham, as Elbee walked down the aisle with his mother. The camera flashes made Elbee feel like he was a superstar.

Once Elbee was front and center, the first song came to an end. Within seconds, a young lady began to sing *Ribbon in the Sky* by Stevie Wonder. Then the bridal party began to elegantly descend down the spiral staircases that were located on each side of the wedding hall. Everyone oohed and aahed as the bridesmaids and groomsmen came together in front of the audience. Immediately after the bridal party was in place, the doors of the wedding hall were closed.

Elbee turned and took a step towards the center aisle. The

crowd stood and the doors opened up. Standing there with her parents was the most beautiful and elegant bride that Elbee had ever seen.

With the first note the piano player played, Angel began to walk down the aisle.

The soloist began singing, "I've been so many places; seen so many things."

The words of the song caused tears to well up in Angel's eyes. She had heard the song many times while she was with Elbee, and she knew what it meant to him. This was going to be a day to remember.

As Angel continued towards the man of her dreams, she looked around at all of the family and friends who were there to support her. While she scanned the crowd, there was a chill that came over her, but it was short lived as she reached her husband-to-be.

"Dearly beloved, we are gathered here today to join this man and this woman. Who giveth this woman away?"

"I do," Mr. Terry answered.

Once Mr. Terry answered, the minister continued on with the ceremony. Everything was going along just as it had been practiced during the wedding rehearsal.

"Is there anyone here who feels that this man and this woman should not be married? Speak now or forever hold your peace."

She Made Her Bed

Rocky and Tony sat in the back of the wedding as the people filed in. Tony didn't understand why they were there. Rocky had lost all the way around. The police were looking for him and he had no other plans. In Tony's mind, they should have been on their way back to Georgia.

Rocky was in total disbelief. Everything he had done to discredit Elbee and have the wedding called off had failed. He had even tried to get Elbee arrested as a suspect for Tasha's murder. That didn't work because Elbee was with the Chief of Police at a mentoring meeting during the time of the murder. How was that for an alibi?

There had to be a way to stop this wedding, but how? What could he possibly do to stop this madness?

The minister asked, "Is there anyone here who feels that this man and this woman should not be married? Speak now or forever hold your peace."

At that moment, Rocky stood up. "I have a reason."

Everyone in the place turned and looked at Rocky. They were all wondering who this person could be.

Angel couldn't believe what she was hearing. When she turned and saw Rocky, she was speechless. She looked at Blak as if she was asking him for help, but he couldn't help her. Blak was worried about his friendship with Elbee.

Elbee frowned and whispered to DB, "That's the nigga I beat for all that cash last week. I'm gonna fuck this bastard up."

When Elbee started walking towards Rocky, Ricky stepped out into the aisle in front of him.

"Rocky, what are you doing here?" Ricky questioned sternly.

"Pop, is that you?"

When Tony saw that Ricardo was in attendance, he began sliding down in his seat. He was not looking forward to dealing with him. He had seen Ricardo upset before, and it was absolutely brutal.

Looking up at Rocky, all Tony could say was, "Dude, we're in some trouble trouble."

"Yeah, it's me, Rock. Now what the hell are you doing here messing up these people's wedding?"

"Pop, he has something that belongs to me, and I came here to kill him to take it back."

"Am I wrong or did I leave word that he was not to be touched?" Ricardo admonished. "Did Tony not tell you what I said?" he continued, looking at Tony.

"Pop, he has the most precious thing in the world to me, and the only way to get it back is to kill him."

Four of Ricardo's associates stood up. "Rocky, I love you, but there is no way I'm letting you kill my son," Ricardo

Speak Now Or...Hold Your Piece

announced.

Rocky was stunned by this new revelation. His mind became very clear. He now understood why Elbee had so much clout in the streets and why no one was able to touch him. Although the situation was spiraling out of control for him, now wasn't the time for him to back down.

"Well, why is your son getting ready to marry my wife?" Rocky stated matter-of-factly.

Elbee looked at Rocky with fire in his eyes. "Nigga, who are you and what the fuck are you talking about? Is all of this because you lost your rent money to me? Ricky, do you really know this bama?"

"Angel, you didn't tell your husband-to-be that you already have a husband?" Rocky inquired, poking his chest out.

"Angel, what is this dude talking 'bout? Do you know him? Are you married to this guy?" Elbee demanded.

The guests in the hall were astonished. No one had ever seen anything like this before, yet they all sat listening to what was transpiring. Blak stood behind Elbee looking at Carolyn and shaking his head. This is exactly what he didn't want to happen.

Elbee was looking at Angel waiting for her to say something, but to no avail.

"Angel, do you know this muthafucka?" Elbee asked again with anger in his voice.

Angel dropped her head and started to cry, but she still didn't answer. She was waiting for her father to come rescue her, although she knew he wouldn't. He had told her many times that not telling Elbee everything could be detrimental to their relationship, and now it was time for her to deal with the consequence and repercussions of her actions.

"Answer me!" Elbee yelled.

Rocky moved towards Elbee. "Don't you ever yell at my wife again, muthafucka!"

At that moment, the rage in Elbee had built up so much that he threw two punches, hitting Rocky and causing him to hit the floor. Immediately, Tony hopped up to run to Rocky's defense. No matter what the cost, he wasn't going to let him go down by himself. Before he could get to Elbee, the four guys with Ricardo grabbed him.

Ricardo looked at one of the guys and nodded. With that, the men rustled Tony out of the building. From that point on, Rocky was like Patti LaBelle and Michael McDonald, on his own.

Elbee stood looking at Angel. He was still waiting for her to answer him. Angel turned to look at her parents for help. Being the man that he is, her father started to get up and go to her defense.

Mrs. Terry gently touched her husband's arm. "She made her bed."

...Hold Your Piece

Rocky started to laugh when he saw the frustration on Elbee's face. "Baby, you didn't tell pretty boy here about your husband?"

"Shut up, Rocky!" Angel yelled.

"Oooh, so now you wanna talk?" Elbee chimed in sarcastically.

"Elbee, baby, it's not like that," Angel cried. "I was gonna tell you. It was just hard for me."

"It wasn't hard for you to call off the wedding when you found out about my son. So when were you gonna tell me?" Elbee snapped.

"Yeah, baby, when were you gonna tell him?" Rocky fakely whined, while laughing.

"Shut the fuck up!" Blak snarled.

Getting up off the floor, Rocky took a good look at Blak. "I know you. Yeah, you're the nigga that convinced my lil' Angel that she didn't have to satisfy my clients anymore."

Elbee turned and looked at Blak. He was totally speechless.

Angel was not only married, but she turned tricks, too, and Blak, one of his best friends, knew all of this but never told him.

"Blak, you knew Angel was a lying ho and you didn't tell me?" Elbee exclaimed.

"Elbee, it's not like that. If you just let me explain," Angel cried out.

"So now you wanna talk to me? You ain't wanna talk to a nigga when you thought I was lying to you. Now you want me to listen to your skanky ass. You could've told me all this before today, but you didn't. Why? So you could embarrass me in front of your black-ass husband," Elbee responded angrily. "Fuck you, bitch!"

"Make that the last time you call my wife a bitch," Rocky snarled.

"She's a bitch if I say she's one, and you're an even bigger bitch, bitch!" Elbee responded. "Now what, punk?"

Elbee started to move towards Rocky, but before Elbee could get close enough to hit him again, Rocky pulled a 9mm pistol from his back. He had tasted Elbee's power, and he wasn't trying to tangle with him without Tony.

Everyone but Elbee took a step back. Gun or not, he wasn't going to be intimidated. He had been punked enough for one day, and he hadn't seen Ashton Kutcher anywhere.

"Oh, I'm supposed to be scared because you can make a broad turn tricks and you gotta gun? Nigga, please!" Elbee cautioned.

"Rocky, don't do this. Put the gun down, son," Ricardo pleaded.

Benny took a step towards Elbee. At the same time, Blak, DB, and Ramon stepped up. Each one was waiting for the

Speak Now Or...Hold Your Piece

moment to take Rocky down.

"I can't put the gun down, Pops. I came here for my wife, and I'm not leaving without Angel."

"Rocky, I'm not your wife anymore. I'm marrying Elbee."

Rocky moved closer to Elbee and pointed his gun at Elbee's head. "Not if I have anything to do with it."

JR sat and watched as Rocky made threats on his father's life. It took fifteen years for him to meet his father, and he had no intentions on losing him today. He was going to do what he could to protect his father.

"Rocky, if you do this, you know there is nowhere you can hide where I won't find you. None of the contacts you have will hide you," Ricardo told him.

"Yeah, yeah, yeah. Whatever, Pops. This muthafucka been fucking my wife and you comin' at me? That nigga is gonna beg for his life today, and maybe…just maybe…I'll let him live."

Elbee laughed. "Nigga, you must be outta your rabbit-ass mind. You might as well shoot me now, because I would rather die on my feet than beg on my knees."

Benny, DB, and Ramon were slowly moving into attack position. The only way this fool was making it out of the hall was with a well whooped ass.

"Give it up, Rock. You can't make it outta here. You don't have enough bullets," Ricardo advised him.

Rocky grabbed Angel. "Watch me," he said, then shot Ricardo.

The sound of gunshots caused everyone to scramble. Rocky fired off two more shots while trying to get to the door with Angel. Rocky knew the limo was parked out front. If he could just get to it, then he could get out of town.

Rocky was almost at the door, when he turned to fire another shot and tripped over JR who was kneeling near the door. When Rocky fell, he dropped his gun, losing it in the traffic of people running. He hopped back up, quickly kicked JR in the ribs, and scrambled to find his gun.

"Oh hell no! You gonna ruin my wedding and kick my son! Take this, muthafucka!" Elbee shouted, punching Rocky in his face.

Rocky stumbled back into the wall.

"Whoop his ass, El!" Benny yelled as he fought through the crowd trying to get to his cousin.

Rocky tried hard to fight back, but his efforts were futile. The more he fought, the more he got hit. Elbee wasn't showing any signs of letting up. Then it seemed like Elbee was an octopus, because punches were coming from every angle.

Rocky fell to the ground, and Elbee, Benny, DB, Blak, and Ramon began stomping him. Rocky could taste the blood going down his throat as his eyes started to close. He was in unchartered territory. Rocky had stomped a lot of people, but he had never been stomped before. Just as he was about to pass out, he felt the hard, cold steel of his 9mm.

Grabbing the gun, Rocky started firing and bodies began to drop. He could barely see and didn't know who he was shooting. All he knew was he needed to get outside.

Rocky turned to run. Not knowing who to trust, he just shot. With his vision clearing, he could see that he had shot Angel. Bodies were on the ground and people were still running around. Rocky could see Ricardo still lying on the floor, and he knew he had to get out of DC.

Speak Now Or...Hold Your Piece

When Rocky turned to run, he was shot twice in the chest. He dropped to his knees and let his gun fall. While he laid there bleeding to death, he could hear the paramedics say the bride didn't make it.

Before he took his last breath, Rocky smiled and uttered, "Til death do us part."

In the News

"In breaking news. Today there was a shooting at a wedding in Temple Hills, Maryland. Reports say an uninvited guest stood up and opposed the nuptials of Elbee Nessprin to Angel Terry and later started shooting. The shooter was identified as Rocky Espanaza, who shot and fatally wounded several people before being killed by police. We will have more information as the story develops," the news anchor reported.